I0452325

When she rejected him, the spell was supposed to break...so why wasn't it?

Part of her wanted to run and hide away so that his words couldn't hurt her, but another part—the witchy, bitchy part—wanted to let him know that it was the sexy Sean who she was turning him down for. Guess which side of her won?

"Actually, Reid, it is Sean that I'm seeing. On Monday night he confessed that he had started having feelings for me and that he had never realized that I had feelings for him. As you said yourself, I've had a crush on him forever, so I'm sure you can understand why I would want to see where this thing with him could go."

Why wasn't the spell breaking?

Hank was holding out her coat, so Maddy got up, put it on, and started gathering her things. She guessed Hank didn't think she was going to be able to rationalize with Reid and he was probably right. The spell didn't seem to be breaking and Reid didn't seem to be understanding that she didn't want to go out with him because there was someone else. Maddy really needed to talk to Fiona and see where she was on finding a spell to break the Make Me a Match spell. That might be the only way to deal with Reid.

Tired of kissing frogs, Maddy Simpson finds her family's spell book and casts the Make Me a Match Spell, trying to lure her Prince Charming. But something goes terribly wrong. Instead of capturing the interest of her one true love, she attracts all the men in town, both young and old, married or single. The spell is easily broken once Maddy rejects the men, but one man just won't take no for an answer. Oops. Now Maddy has to find a way to get rid of him, while also figuring out if the love she has found with her best friend—and longtime crush—is real or just a result of the spell.

KUDOS for *Make Me a Match*

In *Make Me a Match* by Carrie Zimmerman, Maddy is a witch—a witch in love with Sean, who thinks of her as just a friend. He also doesn't know she's a witch. In desperation, Maddy uses a spell to help her find her true love and get over Sean as he is never going to return her feelings. When she says the spell she is supposed to think about what she wants in a man. Instead, she is so worried about saying the words right that she forgets to think about what her dream man. Thus, the spell is non-specific and applies to all men, not just the one she wants. As a result Maddy suddenly becomes extremely popular. Men from 19 to 99 are asking her out. Maddy is frantically trying to figure out how to undo the spell, when Sean decides that he loves her after all. But does he really, or is he just reacting to the spell? The story is very clever and the characters enchanting. The plot is fresh and unique, with some nice surprises to keep you on your toes. ~ *Taylor Jones, Reviewer*

Match Me a Match revolves around Maddy, who's a witch, but not a very skilled one. She is tired of pining away for the man she loves—who doesn't return her feelings—so she decides to use a spell to find her true love. Did I mention that she is not particularly skilled? Well, you guessed it, she screws up. Instead of attracting her dream man, she attracts everyone. So what's wrong with that? you ask. Well, this means she attracts eighty-year-old married seniors as well psychos—yes, it's a major oops. The characters are charming and well-developed. The plot is strong, and quite clever. While there are a number of books out there about witches and spells, there are too many about bumbling ones who mess up their spells. This gives Zimmerman's tale a fresh and unique twist that only adds to its appeal. This light-hearted fantasy romance is guaranteed to make you laugh, cry, and gasp, sometimes on the same page. *~ Regan Murphy, Reviewer*

ACKNOWLEDGEMENTS

A big thank you to my husband and children for helping me believe in myself and not give up on the dream of becoming a published author. I couldn't have done this without the four of you.

Thank you to the Black Opal Books team. I have loved working with all of you and hope that we work together again.

Make Me A Match

Carrie Zimmerman

A Black Opal Books Publication

Black Opal Books

BECAUSE SOME STORIES JUST HAVE TO BE TOLD

GENRE: FANTASY ROMANCE/PARANORMAL ROMANCE

This is a work of fiction. Names, places, characters and incidents are either the product of the author's imagination or are used fictitiously, and any resemblance to any actual persons, living or dead, businesses, organizations, events or locales is entirely coincidental. All trademarks, service marks, registered trademarks, and registered service marks are the property of their respective owners and are used herein for identification purposes only. The publisher does not have any control over or assume any responsibility for author or third-party websites or their contents.

MAKE ME A MATCH
Copyright © 2015 by Carrie Zimmerman
Cover Design by Jackson Cover Design
All cover art copyright © 2015
All Rights Reserved
Print ISBN: 978-1-626942-61-5

First Publication: APRIL 2015

All rights reserved under the International and Pan-American Copyright Conventions. No part of this book may be reproduced or transmitted in any form or by any means, electronic or mechanical, including photocopying, recording, or by any information storage and retrieval system, without permission in writing from the publisher.

WARNING: The unauthorized reproduction or distribution of this copyrighted work is illegal. Criminal copyright infringement, including infringement without monetary gain, is investigated by the FBI and is punishable by up to 5 years in federal prison and a fine of $250,000.

ABOUT THE PRINT VERSION: If you purchased a print version of this book without a cover, you should be aware that the book is stolen property. It was reported as "unsold and destroyed" to the publisher, and neither the author nor the publisher has received any payment for this "stripped book."

IF YOU FIND AN EBOOK OR PRINT VERSION OF THIS BOOK BEING SOLD OR SHARED ILLEGALLY, PLEASE REPORT IT TO: lpn@blackopalbooks.com

Published by Black Opal Books **http://www.blackopalbooks.com**

DEDICATION

For Erik, my very own romance hero.
(Next time you'll be on the cover...I promise)

Chapter 1

Walking through the aisles of Full Moon Books was like visiting old friends for Maddy Simpson. She spent more time there than she did at home, so immediately upon finding an unfamiliar book, she was more than a little curious. Maddy carefully picked up the book and carried it back to her office.

The book felt familiar in a way a book shouldn't—like a living, breathing thing instead of a collection of paper and ink. The book smelled like cinnamon, cloves, and the past. For an instant, Maddy was transported to her grandmother's kitchen, watching her stir some mysterious potion. Maddy ran her hand along the faded cover, feeling the embedded pattern that had faded to the point of being indistinguishable from the leather. Maddy opened the book and gasped.

There on the very first page, written in what looked like either dark red ink, or maybe blood, was a protection spell, marking the book as something only those in the direct line of the Simpson witches would be able to hold or read. This was the Simpson spell book and it should have been packed away in her attic. *How did it get to the bookstore?*

Maddy started to flip to the next page when her office door flew open.

"Maddy, you have to see—" Annie, her college-aged weekend helper, came bursting through. Maddy quickly shut the book and covered it with a stack of papers from her desk. Annie stopped and took a deep breath. "You have to come and look at this guy who's looking around in the thriller section. He is the hottest damn thing I've seen in a very long time."

As quickly as she had burst into Maddy's office, Annie was gone, but she wouldn't leave Maddy alone if there was a sexy man involved, so Maddy carefully wrapped the spell book up in a sweatshirt she kept in her office and put it into her tote bag. Maddy's cousin Fiona would know what to do with the misplaced book and might even know how it had managed to appear at Full Moon Books.

As nonchalantly as possible, Maddy walked to the

front of the store, pausing here and there to arrange books on shelves or to see if a customer needed help. She made it close to the thriller section before pausing to look for the man Annie had been drooling over in her office. She froze when she saw him. *Damn, he's one sexy man.*

For a moment Maddy's brain took a detour to fantasy land and she imagined herself walking straight up to the sexy stranger, pulling him close, and kissing him. It had been more than a year since she had gone on a date and the lack of mouth to mouth contact with a man was start-ing to get to her. She shook her head to chase the fantasy away and took another look at the man. He was really gorgeous. He had reddish brown hair, freckles, and in-credible cheekbones. Maddy had never been attracted to a man with red hair before, but this man was sex on a stick.

Annie sidled up beside Maddy and poked her in the ribs. "Why don't you see if he needs any help?"

Maddy smiled. "Why don't you?"

"He's too old for me and I've got a man. But I checked and there's no ring on his finger."

"Just because there's no ring doesn't mean he's sin-gle, Annie."

"No, but he's looked over here several times while we've been talking and I think he's been checking out your ass."

Maddy laughed, but was secretly pleased. She chanced another look over at Mr. Sexy and, sure enough, he was looking right at her. He smiled her way and she smiled back. Just as Maddy was gathering her courage to go talk to the gorgeous stranger her cell phone rang. *Thank you, universe.*

While flirting with Mr. Sexy held appeal, Maddy really wanted to get back to the spell book and find out exactly who, what, where, and how she was going to deal with whatever chaos it was sure to unleash. Because Maddy knew one thing—nothing good ever came from a Simpson witch messing with magic.

Chapter 2

The moment Fiona walked in the door of the house they shared, Maddy grabbed her by the hand and pulled her to the family room.

"Maddy, you're hurting me." Fiona shook off Maddy's hand. "What's going on with you?"

Maddy walked over to the sofa and sat down heavily. She didn't know where to start explaining to Fiona what had happened to her that day or how she felt like she was losing her mind just a bit. She sighed. "Sit down and I'll try and explain."

Fiona took a seat beside her as Maddy took the book off of the coffee table and placed it in her lap. The book vibrated with power as she held it in her hands.

"This is what has me so worked up."

Fiona gasped. "Maddy, that's the Simpson spell book."

She started to grab it out of Maddy's hands, but Maddy couldn't let her touch the book. It was hers. "Yes, it is. Have you seen it before?"

"Grandmother showed it to me before she passed away. How do you have it?"

"I found it on a shelf in the rare book section at the store. I have no idea how it got there, but it makes me feel crazy possessive and out of sorts. You have to help me figure out how it got out of the attic and what I'm supposed to do with it."

Maddy had always kept her distance from witchcraft. She had mastered a few easy spells as a child and some more complicated ones as a teen, but she was more of an Aunt Clara than a Samantha. Fiona had loved all of the witchy stuff and had continued learning from their grandmother long after Maddy gave up. She could probably turn some guy into a toad, which now that Maddy thought about it, would be a great skill to learn.

"You're probably meant to find a spell," Fiona said as if that made complete sense. "Grandmother spelled the book before she passed so it would find us when we needed it. I've been waiting, but I guess you needed the book first."

Fiona stared at the book with longing and disappointment on her face. Maddy wished the book had found her cousin first. Maddy needed Fiona's help, so hopefully that would ease some of the disappointment her cousin was sure to be feeling. "You have to help me. I don't know what I could need that is in this book, but you know so much more about this stuff. You have to help me figure it out. Pretty please, say you will."

Fiona leaned over and gave her a big hug. "Of course, I will help you. We need to relax and look through the book. According to Grandmother, you will just know when you find whatever it is you are supposed to find in the book. We should order a pizza, change into our pajamas, and open a bottle of wine. This book is huge and who knows how long it will take us to find the page you are supposed to find."

"Oh, Fi, I knew you would come up with a plan."

They shared a pizza, drank a bottle and a half of wine, and looked through the spell book together, laughing at the spells they read. There were spells for finding lost objects, cleaning house, and getting a tan.

"Maybe I should have focused more on what Grandmother was trying to teach me. It would be fantastic to start swimsuit season with a perfect tan just by mumbling a few words," Maddy said.

"Grandmother always told us we shouldn't do spells for personal gain."

"Like the Haliwell sisters on Charmed?"

Fiona laughed. "Something like that but, on more than one occasion, I saw Grandmother use a spell to clean the kitchen or even to spell up a new outfit."

Maddy emptied her wine glass and smiled. "It's too bad we haven't found a spell to magically refill our wine glasses or at least make another bottle appear."

"I'll go get another bottle—you keep reading. We've made it through a little more than half the book. We have to find the spell soon."

Thanks to another two glasses of wine, Maddy was feeling nice and fuzzy when, out of nowhere, she felt a sudden sharp pain flow through her whole body, as if she had been stunned by a Taser. "Son of a bitch."

Fiona jumped up, spilling her glass of wine. "What?"

"I was just shocked." Maddy looked at the spell book and felt the shock again, but this time it wasn't as strong. There at the top of the page was the name of the spell she had been destined to find. "This is it, Fiona, what I was meant to find in this huge, crazy book."

The Make Me a Match spell was on page 1569 of the Simpson Family Spell Book. Fiona and Maddy just stared at it.

"A matchmaking spell?" Fiona asked, surprised.

"Yep."

"Huh."

The cousins sat and starred at the book some more before actually reading what was written on the page. After Maddy finished reading the spell, she started laughing. "So I do this spell and it makes the dude I desire, desire me?"

Fiona started laughing too. "Dude?"

"I don't know what I'm saying anymore. Between the wine, the weirdness of the book turning up, and learning my dead grandmother somehow thinks I need a spell to get me a man—I'm losing it. Is the word dude really that wrong? What word should I use—stud, macho-macho-man, sex-toy, object of my desire?"

"Calm down, Maddy. Your voice is doing that thing where it goes up three octaves. You are getting very close to a freak out. I don't know what's going on either, but I think what the spell does is match you with your true love, whoever that person may be. It says you should clear your mind and think about the qualities of your perfect mate."

Maddy stared at her cousin. "You aren't seriously suggesting I should do this, are you?" Maddy couldn't believe Fiona would think casting a spell to get a man was a good idea.

"I think you have to. That's why the book found you."

"I'm not sure. I don't do this magic stuff and I don't think it's a good idea to mess with stuff you aren't used to messing with." Maddy's head was starting to hurt. She didn't want to get a man just because he was spelled into loving her. "Would you do it if you were me, Fiona?"

"I would, but I believe in all of this hocus pocus."

"I know, but I really don't want to spend my life wondering if the man I'm with really loves me or if he's just under some spell."

"Maddy, I also believe in destiny. I think the person you end up with would have found his way to you, eventually, but this will jump start your epic love story."

"What if it all goes wrong? Is there some magical undo button?"

Fiona shook her head. "Um, no. But usually there is some sort of spell to counteract the original. We would just have to find it. I don't think it will be an issue though. This is a pretty straight forward spell. As long as you are thinking about the qualities you want in a man and not focusing on any one man you will be fine."

Maddy had spent most of the last two years staying at home every Friday night.

It wasn't that she didn't want to date, but she had been hung up on one unobtainable guy for so long that she didn't even know where to start. Her entire twenties had been spent waiting for Sean Walker to realize she was the one for him. They were best friends, had been since high school, and although she would do anything for him to look at her as someone other than a friend, he never had.

"Okay." Maddy took a deep breath. "I'm going to do

this. But first, let's make a list of the qualities so I can focus on it while I cast the spell."

Fiona grabbed a piece of paper and started writing as Maddy started listing the qualities she looked for in a man out loud. "He needs to have a great sense of humor, be taller than me, have blue eyes, be intelligent, and in his thirties. He also needs to love old movies and to read. Dimples and an understanding of my irrational love of coffee wouldn't hurt either."

"I'm not trying to start anything, but you do know you just described Sean, don't you?"

"Yes, Fiona, but I'm sure it also described other men in Hollow Moon too," Maddy said while rolling her eyes.

Fiona pulled the spell book closer to her and reread the spell. "Now, you have to cast the spell while thinking about those qualities and nothing else. You can't focus on any one man in particular." Fiona looked at Maddy with a critical eye. "Do you think you can do the spell tonight or should we wait until the morning when you aren't...well, drunk?"

Waiting till morning was probably the responsible thing to do, but Maddy was afraid if she waited until she was sober she would chicken out. "I'm fine, Fiona. Let's do this!"

With Fiona standing by her side, Maddy stood in front of the book and blinked several times. The words wavered a bit, but Maddy wasn't going to let a little bit of fear stop her.

She began to recite the words of the spell three times:

"Make me a match so I will know the delight in a kiss, the bliss in a touch, and the promise of forever. Make me a match so I will know the delight in a kiss, the bliss in a touch, and the promise of forever. Make me a match so I will know the delight in a kiss, the bliss in a touch, and the promise of forever."

Maddy finished and looked at Fiona. "Is that it?"

"I guess. Do you feel different?"

"No?" Maddy didn't feel any different than she had an hour earlier, except she was starting to get a bit of a headache from all of the wine she'd drunk. Then it hit her. "Shit."

"What?"

Maddy felt her stomach fall to her toes. "I was thinking so hard about saying the words in the right order I didn't think about the qualities I wanted in a man. I didn't think about anything but the words I was saying. What's going to happen?"

Fiona shrugged her shoulders. "I guess we'll find out."

Chapter 3

Sean Walker had spent the last twelve years living away from Hollow Moon and he was ready to move back home. He loved his life in Boston, but the last few months had left him feeling restless. During college, he had started a website connecting adults with tutors to help them improve in areas that would help them advance in the job market. It had started as a class project and, in a few years, grown into a multi-million dollar company with multiple educational websites.

Six months ago he had sold the company and was now at a loss for what to do next. He didn't need to work, but after several months of sitting around trying to find something to fill the hours and two vacations by himself,

he had learned that a life of leisure wasn't for him. Between talking to his sister, Cassidy; his best friend, Hank;
and his friend, Maddy, Sean was homesick.

He wanted to be able to see the people whose lives
he knew so much about but didn't take an active role in.
When Hank called him, freaking out because Cassidy had
a hangover, Sean wanted to be able to laugh about it with
her.

Hank might even calm down about his role as her
protector if Sean came back home. He was playing Candy
Crush on-line when his phone rang and the caller ID
showed it was Cassidy. Smiling, he answered the phone.
"Hey, sis."

"Hey, big brother. Are you super busy watching TV
or playing on-line?"

Sean laughed. She constantly gave him a hard time
about having nothing to do. "I was playing Candy Crush,
but thinking about how I could take over the world."

"Well, at least you are planning something. Seriously, are you going to do something soon or just live the life
of the idle rich and do nothing?"

"It's funny you should ask. I've been considering
what I want to do next and I'm thinking about moving
home." Cassidy's squeal of joy was so loud he had to pull
the phone away from his ear. "I'm guessing that would
make you happy?"

"Sean, you're not joking with me, are you?"

"Nope. I have a few ideas for a new start-up, but I don't think I want to do them here in Boston. Since they are Internet based too, I can do them anywhere."

"I know everyone would love to have you back and I'm sure Hank would let you work at the coffee shop. You know, if you really are a washed up hack with no more ideas and need a job."

"Very funny," he said, even though there was a small part of him worried she wasn't far from the truth. "So anything new happening in Hollow Moon?"

"Maddy's dating."

Sean sighed. Cassidy was always telling him things about Maddy because she had it in her head there was more between them then just a really close friendship. Sure, he knew Maddy was gorgeous and a time or two he had thought about kissing her and what it would be like if they took their relationship to another level, but they never would. Maddy didn't think of him that way and, even if she did, it wouldn't be worth the risk of losing one of his best friends for a short lived romantic relationship. "That's great." Wasn't it?

"I guess. It's just kind of weird. Maddy has never really dated and, all of a sudden, she's got like three dates lined up with different guys. I'm not sure what's going on with her."

"I don't know either, Cass. The last time I called her we only talked for five minutes before she had to go."

Which now that he thought about it wasn't like Maddy at all either. Usually their phone calls went on for hours unless he had something going on. Maddy was someone he could always depend on being there for him. Maybe he needed to make a trip to Hollow Moon to see what was going on with her. Not because she was dating, she could date whoever she wanted, but because she was acting so out of character. He needed, as a friend, to make sure she was okay—at least that was the story he was going to tell anyone who asked and what he told Cassidy. He made plans with her to come to Hollow Moon the next weekend and look for a place to live when he moved back home.

Chapter 4

How's Miss Popular today?" Fiona asked, as she walked into the kitchen.

"I'm not sure I can go to work. People are starting to notice I'm hot stuff all of a sudden and I don't know if I can explain it away or if I should pretend I don't know what anyone is talking about." Maddy had buried her face in her arms on the kitchen table so the words were slightly muffled and she knew she sounded pitiful. "It wasn't supposed to be this way, Fiona. Prince Charming was supposed to come and sweep me off my feet and we would live happily ever after. I wasn't supposed to attract the attention of everyone in town with a Y chromosome."

Fiona walked over to her and wrapped her arms around Maddy's shoulders. "I know, Maddy. I'm trying to find some way to reverse the spell. Just be grateful—so far it seems to break easily. But a few of the guys who've asked you out haven't been awful. You said yes to Jason, Mike, and Steve."

She raised her head and smiled "I did, although my date with Jason was terrible. I'm trying. I just need to suck it up and go to work."

She retreated to her bedroom where she pulled out her clothes for work. Yesterday, she had dressed a little dowdier than she usually did, in slacks and a big sweater. But today she was going back to her normal way of dressing.

She pulled out a blue skirt, white sweater, and blue heels. She did her makeup the way she always did and put on her jewelry. She wanted to look good if she ran into Mr. Right.

She walked back out into the living room and Fiona whistled. "You look good today."

"Thanks. I decided not to hide away like I did yesterday. I want to look good if I meet someone who is actually eligible. There has to be some advantage to this stupid spell. I have to meet at least one or two men I would want to go out with, right? I can think of ten guys in town I would say yes to if they asked me out, but I haven't run into them."

"Maybe you need to make sure you run into them. Name a couple of guys on your list."

"Declan Moore, of course, Reid Mitchell, and maybe Hank," she said while gathering up her tote bag and purse. She hated discussing this as if it was some type of strategy session for a war.

"Hank Colburn, Sean's best friend, is someone you might want to date?"

"Um, well, he's hot, nice, and I know we get along. I've never let myself think of him as anything other than Sean's best friend, but I think he and I would click." She had meditated long and hard about whom she could see herself with from town, and Hank was definitely someone she could see herself with.

"I can see you two together. I just didn't think about it because of the Sean connection. You are trying to let your crush on Sean go, aren't you?"

"Yes, I am," Maddy said the words with a conviction she definitely didn't feel. She wanted to let go of her crush on Sean Walker, but how did you turn off something that had been a part of you for the last fifteen years? It wasn't like there was a button she could push. Maybe there was a spell? The idea of combing through *that* book again freaked her out, but if there was some magical shut-off valve for her feelings for Sean, maybe she should look at it.

Then she could date and find someone else and be

happy without the "what ifs" constantly playing in her head while she was on these dates with these perfectly great guys.

Maddy walked into her bookstore, feeling a little better than she had the day before. She knew what to do when she was hit on and she had a plan, of sorts, to get noticed by the types of men she wanted to notice her. But what she wanted to do was forget she had even cast the ridiculous spell.

She put her stuff in her office and, since it was Tuesday and new books were releasing, she made sure everything had made it onto the sales floor the night before. They might be a small town bookstore, but if she didn't have the newest romance novels out front and center, her great-aunt, Miss May, would let her have it. Everything was where it was supposed to be, so she went back into her office to do some paperwork.

But before she made it to the back there was a knocking at the window. She looked out and there stood Jasper Wilkins, the sixty-three year old married man who ran the town newspaper.

She had a feeling he wasn't there to ask her for something to do with an article or advertising, but she couldn't just ignore the man.

She walked to the door and unlocked it to let him in. Jasper immediately walked in and pulled her into his arms. "Maddy, darling."

He leaned in to kiss her and she screamed, "Jasper Wilkins, you let go of me this second. I do not want to kiss you."

A shiver went through Jasper's body and he looked at her with confusion. "Hi, Maddy. Were we meeting this morning?"

She didn't know what to say. "Um, I just wanted to ask you if you had read the newest, um, James Patterson book."

He gave her an odd look, but didn't seem to think her question was too out of character. "I don't think I have."

"Well, I only have one more copy and I wouldn't want you to miss it. It was fantastic." At least she had heard it was. She was strictly a romance and self-help reader.

"I guess I better get it then. I do like his Alex Cross books."

She sighed in relief. The spell had broken and Mr. Wilkins didn't seem to have any ill effects from being momentarily crazy about her. She found the book and sold it to him. Well, that was one thing she could do. She could hand-sell a book to every man who hit on her. When the spell broke, she would tell them they had been discussing a book and they were going to buy it. Full Moon Books could make a little money off of the Make Me a Match spell.

Mr. Wilkins left and she went to her office. Her determination to make the best out of her bad situation was no longer as strong. She had just been accosted by someone old enough to be her grandfather. It was too much to take.

An hour later all of her book orders had been entered in, her bills paid, and anything else she could do in order to remain hiding in her office accomplished. It was time to open the store and face the good people of Hollow Moon—and hope she saw more female customers than male.

The bell over the door dinged as it opened. She looked up and took a deep breath. It was him. Mr. Sexy from the previous Saturday. He was gorgeous. Ginger hair, high cheekbones, and striking blue eyes. He wore a suit and tie and looked like he had stepped out of a magazine ad. Now was her chance to let the spell do its magic and get her a date with someone she did desire.

"Welcome to Full Moon Books. I'm Maddy. Is there something I can help you find today?"

He smiled at her and she swore her knees went weak for a second. "Nice to meet you, Maddy. I'm Declan Moore. I just moved to Hollow Moon to take over Mr. Simon's law practice." He held out his hand to shake hers and, as she placed her hand in his, there were some definite sparks. "I was hoping you might have a copy of the latest Grisham or Patterson?"

"Well, you're in luck because I have both." She led

him over to where the books were located and handed him both books. "I didn't know Mr. Simon was retiring."

"His wife, who is my mother's sister, told him he was retiring."

They both laughed. "I can see Mrs. Simon doing that. I know she wanted to travel and to visit their grandkids more. She bought copies of almost every travel guide I had, but she never said they were, in truth, going."

"They have gone. I moved into their house, temporarily, last week and took over the cases my uncle still had open. There were only two. He said he mainly does estate planning and stuff like that."

"Hollow Moon is a great place, unless you are looking for a lot of hustle and bustle. We don't have that here."

"I'm not looking for any hustle or bustle. I've been practicing law in Dallas and was quickly getting burnt out. I needed a break and when Uncle Jonas asked me if I would consider taking over his practice, I jumped on it. I've always liked the idea of settling in a smaller town."

They had walked over to the cash register as they talked, so she rang his books up and they completed the transaction.

"I'm glad I came in here this morning," he said as he put his credit card back in his wallet.

"I'm happy I had the books you were looking for,"

she said with a smile. She had enjoyed talking to Declan, but was confused he hadn't immediately asked her out. The last few days it had seemed most of the men she had come upon had instantly acted on their attraction.

"I have a confession to make," Declan said with a sheepish grin.

"What?"

"I wasn't really looking for these books. I saw you through the window and had to come meet you. I used the books as an excuse. I read all my books on my tablet and I've already read these."

She didn't know what to say. She was flattered he came up with an excuse to meet her and a tiny bit irritated he admitted to her he didn't buy real books.

"I know that makes me sound a little crazy, but I promise you I'm not. I just looked through the window and saw a beautiful woman I wanted to meet. I didn't even know you owned the store when I came in. You could have been a customer. I'm not making myself sound any better, am I?" They both laughed and some of the tension broke. "Maddy, would you go out with me. To dinner or a movie?"

Without any thought, she said, "I would love to, De-clan."

"Tonight?"

"Okay."

"I can pick you up at your place or—"

"Why don't you pick me up here at six? That's when we close."

"Sounds like a plan. I will see you at six o'clock tonight." Declan kissed her cheek and was walking out the door at the exact same moment that Cassidy was walking in with her morning caffeine and pastry fix. He held the door open for her, but didn't pay any extra attention to her. It was reassuring he didn't do the normal double take most men did. Cassidy was a knockout—blond hair, blue eyes and a killer figure. Most men couldn't help but hit on Cassidy, especially when she turned on the smile like she did for Declan.

"Who was that?" Cassidy asked as she handed over the venti mocha and apple fritter from Crescent Coffee where she worked.

"Declan Moore, Hollow Moon's newest lawyer, and my date for tonight," Maddy said with just a hint of pride.

"You have a date? With him?"

"There's no need to sound so shocked, Cassidy. I'm not an ogre." She was a little hurt that Cassidy found it so unbelievable she would have a date with someone as gorgeous as Declan. Of course, this date was probably due to the influence of the Make Me a Match spell.

"Don't be stupid. I didn't mean it that way and you know it. I'm jealous."

"I'm nervous. He's gorgeous. I don't know what I should wear."

"I can help with that," Cassidy assured her.

They spent the rest of Cassidy's break figuring out what Maddy would wear and how long it would take her to get ready. Fiona came in to work that afternoon at the bookstore at two o'clock, so if Maddy left then, she would have plenty of time to go home and get ready.

"Oh, I had something I needed to talk with you about and I completely forgot in all of the Declan date goodness," Cassidy said.

"What?"

"It's about Sean," Cassidy said, wrinkling her nose, which was a dead giveaway to those that knew her that she had something big to tell and was worried about how the other person was going to take the news.

"Okay, Cassidy. You better spit it out. Hank isn't going to be thrilled you've been gone for twenty minutes. If you're gone any longer, he's going to start calling."

"I know." Cassidy took a deep breath. "Sean's coming home."

"For the weekend? We'll have to get together and go to the Blood Moon." Maddy's heart began beating faster at the idea of seeing Sean. She could pretend it wouldn't affect her at all, but the truth was that even hearing his name made the butterflies in her tummy dance. Seeing him in person would make it a lot harder to get over her crush.

"No, not just for the weekend. Well, for the weekend

right now, but he is moving back to Hollow Moon."

"Really?"

"Yes, he told me yesterday. He said he had been thinking about it for a while, but had made up his mind over the weekend. He said it was time for him to come back home."

"I bet you are thrilled at the idea of having your brother back and Hank is glad to not have to play watch-dog over you anymore."

"Yes, but what do *you* think about Sean coming back to Hollow Moon, Maddy?"

What *did* she think about Sean coming back? It was a good question. Maddy was thrilled he would be back in town. They had been friends for a very long time and she would love to be able to see him all the time instead of just talking over the phone. Her crush on him was another matter.

She had long thought Sean was the perfect man for her, but he had never noticed her as anything other than a friend. When he had left for college, she had told herself she had to get over him, but it hadn't been easy. In fact, she hadn't been able to do it. She still thought they would be perfect together. "I think it's great. You know Sean and I still talk on the phone a lot. I'm not as wrapped up in him as you seem to think. If I was, would I be dating and going out with Declan?"

"I guess not," Cassidy said. "I gotta go back, Hank's

going to kill me for being gone so long." She left the bookstore and Maddy stood staring after her. Why did Sean have to come back now?

Chapter 5

Maddy made it back to the bookstore with fifteen minutes to spare before Declan was supposed to pick her up. She had taken a bath, painted her nails a gorgeous silver color, and put her hair up in hot rollers. She felt relaxed and pretty. The dress she had chosen to wear for the date was tighter than what she usually wore and showed way more cleavage, thanks to her miracle bra. When one was going on a date with such a sexy guy, you really had to try your hardest to look hot.

"Damn, Maddy."

Hank Colburn, Sean's best friend and one of the men from her list, stopped her before she could go into the bookstore. She hadn't thought about what would happen when other men saw her while she was on her date with Declan. Oh, this could be terrible. What if she spent the whole night dealing with other men hitting on her? There was no way Declan would want to go out with her again if she attracted attention from other men all night—or maybe he would. Men were weird.

"You look amazing."

"Thanks, Hank."

He twirled his fingers in the universal signal for her to spin around and she obliged. "Maddy, would you go out with me?"

She was stunned by the suddenness of his question. "Like to lunch?"

"Or the movies or something?"

She wasn't sure what to say, but she knew she didn't want to say no to Hank. "I would love to. I have plans tonight, but I will call you."

Hank smiled and walked back toward his coffee shop.

Maybe being a man magnet wasn't such a bad thing when it was the sexy guys hitting on you all the time. She walked into the bookstore and found Cassidy and Fiona staring at her. "Did you just agree to a date with Hank Colburn?"

"Um, I guess I did." Maddy blushed. "Why?"

"Aren't you already going out on a date?" Fiona asked.

"Tonight, which I told Hank, and said I would call him when I knew I was free. He wanted to go to a movie or something."

Cassidy was just staring at her, so Maddy asked her, "Do you have a problem with me going out with Hank?"

"Not really, I'm just surprised after what I told you about Sean that you are going to go out with his best friend." Cassidy looked thoughtful. "Unless this is some way to make Sean jealous."

"Of course not! I can't believe you would think I would do that. I'm just trying to move on—like we talked about earlier. Hank is a great looking guy, we get along, and I feel comfortable going out with him. It has nothing to do with Sean or his coming back to Hollow Moon."

"Sean's coming home?" Fiona squeaked.

Cassidy nodded her head. "Yes, I told Maddy earlier. He's decided to move back home and he's coming in this weekend to look for a place to live. He's going to stay with Hank." She gave Maddy a look.

Fiona turned to Maddy. "Does this change anything for you and your plan to date and move on?"

Maddy shrugged. "No. It doesn't change anything. I just want to find someone and be happy." And she would keep repeating that to herself over and over until it was the truth.

Declan came into the store at that moment and all three women sighed.

"Hello, Maddy," he said as he handed her a bouquet of roses. "You look amazing."

"Thank you, Declan. You look great too." And boy did he ever. Tonight he was wearing black pants with a white button down shirt. No tie or jacket. He looked half undressed, compared to how she had seen him in the morning, and it made her a little squishy inside.

"I made reservations at a little place in Austen. Shall we go?"

"Okay. Just let me give these flowers to my cousin and grab my purse."

She turned to Fiona and laughed when she saw the look on Fiona and Cassidy's faces. They looked as if they were the ones who had been put under a spell. "Fiona, will you take these home for me?"

Fiona nodded and took the flowers from her. Cassidy leaned in close and whispered, "Go get him, Tiger."

Maddy laughed as she walked back over to Declan. "Are you ready?" she asked.

They left the bookstore and got into Declan's car—a very sexy Ferrari—and headed toward Austin.

"Have you lived in Hollow Moon your whole life?" he asked as they drove.

"No, I moved to Hollow Moon when I was four after my parents died and I came to live with my grandmother.

My parents lived in Dallas when I was born and I lived there until they passed, but I don't really remember it. Hollow Moon is really the only place I remember living."

"I'm not sure I could have lived my whole life in such a small town. I like the idea of living here for a while and slowing down for a bit, but I don't think I will make it more than a year or two."

"I can't imagine living anywhere else. I have the bookstore, plus my friends and family. Hollow Moon is home."

They talked about normal first date things for the rest of their date—favorite music, movies, books. Declan might have a pretty face, but he wasn't someone she had anything in common with at all. They didn't like any of the same things and throughout the date he kept making little statements about Hollow Moon and the people he had met since living there. She guessed it was true that you couldn't judge a book by the cover or a person by their appearance. Declan might look like a gift from heaven, but he really wasn't a nice guy underneath.

He took her home and walked her to the door. Maddy knew she would have to discourage him at this point unless he too picked up on the fact they were incompatible.

"I had a great time tonight, Maddy," he said while leaning in close.

So, he hadn't picked up on the fact this wouldn't

work. "Me too, Declan," she lied. It was so unfair she hadn't had a better time with a man who looked so good. A little voice in her head said to ignore how much she really didn't like him and just make out with him a bit, but she wasn't going to listen to the slutty side of herself.

He reached up to put a lock of hair behind her ear. "I would like to see you again, Maddy."

She took a step back. "Declan, I just don't think that would be a good idea. I had a nice time tonight, but I don't think a relationship between us would make any sense and going on another date would just be a waste of both our time. I'm sorry."

Maddy didn't wait to see what he said in response. She opened the front door, which was thankfully un- locked, and went inside. She stood by the front door until she heard Declan's car leave the driveway.

Fiona came down the stairs and Maddy motioned for her to follow her into the kitchen.

"How was your date?"

"It was okay, but there won't be a second."

"Why not?"

"We had absolutely nothing in common and I didn't see the point in wasting my time or his."

"It might be worth it to just look at him though."

Maddy laughed. "It might, but that's not what I'm looking for and you know that."

"I know, but do you think maybe learning Sean is

coming back to Hollow Moon changed how you felt about your date?" Fiona wasn't one to skate around an issue.

"Um, no, I don't think so. I will admit to being a little curious about what will happen when he comes back, but I don't think he is going to sweep me up into his arms so we can start our wonderful love affair."

"Well, at least you don't have your hopes set high," Fiona said with a laugh. "I just meant I don't want you to turn away from something that could be great because you are still thinking about what could be with Sean."

"I'm not doing that. I honestly had nothing in common with Declan and it would have been a waste of time. A fun waste of time, but a waste just the same."

Chapter 6

Sean drove into Hollow Moon at ten o'clock the following Saturday, smiling at how nothing ever changed in his home town. Everything looked the same as it always had and it made him breathe easier.

There was something reassuring when everything was as he remembered it. Sean had felt a bit panicked this morning as he had left his hotel to make this final part of his journey. What if he felt as trapped in Hollow Moon now as he had as a teenager? He had been sure he was past those feelings now that he had proven to himself and the world he could make it on his own.

He drove down Main Street and parked his car in front of Crescent Coffee. Cassidy was at work and Hank was probably giving her a hard time for whatever she had gotten up to the night before. Sean would surprise his sister and then go to his parents' house for a little bit. He was staying with Hank while he looked for his own place in town.

He didn't think it would take long to find something in Hollow Moon—his choices would be limited but he didn't require much. He parked his Land Rover and got out of the car.

A few people waved and he waved back while taking a deep breath. Maybe it was good to be home.

Walking into the coffee shop put a huge grin on his face. Cassidy was behind the counter helping a customer. He hadn't seen his baby sister in six months and he couldn't wait for her to notice him. There was sure to be screaming and lots of hugging. He walked up to the counter without Cassidy or Hank noticing him.

"What can I get—*Sean*!" Cassidy screamed and was around the counter in three seconds. Sean barely had time to prepare before she was jumping into his arms.

He gave her a big hug and put her down. "Hi, little sister."

"I thought you would go to the parents' house first." She grabbed a hold of his arm and pulled him over to a table while yelling over her shoulder. "Hank, I'm taking another break. Can you please bring my brother a black coffee and I'll take a mocha."

Sean saw Hank roll his eyes, but start to get the coffees ready anyway. His sister still had a way of getting what she wanted where his best friend was concerned. Sean had always thought Hank might have a little crush on Cassidy, but he had always denied it.

"Do you run the place, Cass?"

"Of course," she replied saucily. "So, are you back for good or just a visit?"

"Well, I'll still have to go back to get the rest of my stuff. I was just renting these last couple of months while I decided what to do and I have two months left on my lease, but I gave notice I wasn't renewing. As soon as I find a place here, I will move my stuff."

"I'm so excited you're moving back." Cassidy glanced over at Hank who was making his way over with their coffees. "Maybe you can get my boss to keep his nose out of my personal life," she said, loud enough for Hank to hear.

"Hey, I'm finally closer to having a personal life of my own, so maybe I will keep my nose out of yours," Hank said as he sat down, too. "Breaks over, Cassidy."

"Okay." She gave Sean a kiss on the cheek. "I'll see you later?"

"I was thinking maybe we could all meet up later and hang out somewhere? You, Fiona, Hank—the whole gang." *Maddy.*

But Sean didn't say her name. Ever since their conversation the weekend before, he couldn't get Maddy out of his mind and he thought even including her name on the list would somehow bring attention to his changing feelings for her. Of course, he always included her, so maybe not mentioning her name would put Cassidy on alert.

"Talk to Hank. I'm in and Fiona will be too, but Maddy might have plans. I'll call you later."

Sean turned to Hank. "Are you free tonight?"

Hank laughed. "Since I was planning on you coming in today and you are crashing at my house? Yes, I'm free."

"What was this talk about getting a personal life of your own?"

"Oh, I asked someone out the other day and she said yes. We are going out Monday night."

"Really, is it someone I know or someone who moved to town after I left?"

Hank looked uncomfortable, which Sean thought was odd. He knew it wasn't Cassidy who was the only person Hank would have any reason to feel uncomfortable over asking out as far as Sean was concerned. "It's Maddy, actually."

My Maddy? How was he supposed to feel about his best friends going out on a date? Especially when, all of a sudden, one of those best friends was on his mind all of the time and he kind of wanted her for himself...maybe.

"Maddy Simpson?" *Like there's another Maddy in Hollow Moon.* "I didn't know you liked her."

"Well, I haven't ever really thought of her that way, because she's Maddy, you know. She's gorgeous and funny, but she's always just been part of the crowd. Then the other day she was dressed all up for a date with Declan Moore and I couldn't help but ask her out."

"She was going out with another guy and you asked her out?" That took some balls, Sean thought, and why would Maddy agree to go out with one man when she was on a date with another? Something very odd was going on here.

"Well, I know it doesn't sound good, but it was their first date. I heard from Cassidy it didn't go well and there isn't going to be another. I know she went out last night with Josh from high school, but Cassidy didn't have any idea this morning how her date with him went."

"So, Maddy's dating a lot?" Sean felt like he had landed in some bizarro world. Maddy had never dated much, even when they were in high school. She had always been around when he had found himself dateless on a Friday or Saturday night and they had hung out. Now, it seemed like she was dating every guy in town.

"I guess. I know she's been asked out quite a bit lately. She's always seemed kind of standoffish and like she didn't want to be asked out, but something must have changed because now she is more open to it. I tried to get

information out of Cassidy, but she wouldn't tell me anything. When I asked her about Maddy, she got mad at me
for acting 'like a stupid man who didn't notice someone
until everyone else wanted her' and wouldn't tell me anything."

Sean thought about Maddy. He had never thought
about why she didn't date, but he guessed she didn't really seem to seek out attention from men. Hank was right.
She was gorgeous and fun to hang out with. There was no
reason for her to still be single and it looked like she
wasn't going to be for long. "Well, I'm happy she's having fun." What was a lame thing to say, he thought. How
did he know if she was having fun?

"I hope she's not having too much fun. She might
cancel our date if she really likes one of these other guys
and I wouldn't like that at all."

Sean would, though. He couldn't believe he felt jealous at the idea of Hank going out with Maddy. It was ridiculous. He stood up. "Well, I better go see my parents.
I might stop by and see Maddy and Fiona at the
bookstore."

"Okay. I left a key under the mat at my apartment so
you can let yourself in when you get there if I'm not
home yet."

Sean nodded, waved to Cassidy, and left the coffee
shop. He had planned on going to his parents next, but all
this talk about Maddy and her dating life—and his odd

jealous feelings—made him want to see her for himself. Maybe she had undergone some transformation since the last time he had seen her, making her irresistible to the opposite sex, or maybe it was she was just fantastic and everyone was finally seeing it.

Sean left his car parked in front of Crescent Coffee and walked past the four shops in between it and Full Moon Books. He looked through the window and saw Maddy helping a young teenager look for a book on a display of vampire themed novels. The girl looked thirteen or fourteen and was staring at Maddy as if she was a rock star. Before they could finish their conversation another teenager came walking up, this time a boy, who looked like he was trying to flirt with Maddy.

She must have discouraged him in some way because suddenly his attention turned to the young girl and they started talking about the books Maddy had pointed out. Maddy then ushered them to a group of chairs and the kids sat down together. Maddy turned, shaking her head, and Sean got a full look at her. She was dressed in a sweater dress thing and colored tights with boots that went up to her knees.

Every part of her was covered, but nicely outlined in her form-hugging dress. Her hair was pulled up into a haphazard bun with two pencils through it giving life to a librarian fantasy Sean didn't even know he had. Before he could go in, or even move from where he was staring at her on the sidewalk, Maddy looked up and saw him. His heart skipped a beat and his breath caught. He had never had this sort of reaction to Maddy before. He wanted to walk into the store, pull her into his arms, and place his mouth on hers.

Instead, he unfroze from his place on the sidewalk and walked into Full Moon Books. He kept reminding himself the whole time that this was Maddy Simpson, his friend since school, and not someone he lusted after. He walked right up to her and gave her a friendly hug, in an effort to prove to himself he felt nothing for her but friendship. Friendship and a whole lot of lust.

He quickly took two steps back. "Hi, Maddy."

"Sean! I can't believe you are really back. Cassidy said today was the day, but part of me never really thought you would come back to Hollow Moon. Fiona's in the back, she'll be excited to see you, too."

"I'm really back. I canceled the lease on my place in Boston and everything."

They stood staring at each other for a few awkward seconds. Sean didn't know what to say. This was Maddy. He always knew what to say to Maddy, but for the first time he couldn't think of a thing. Thankfully, Fiona came out from the back of the store then and saw him. "*Sean!*"

Maddy had never been more grateful for her cousin in her whole life. Sean was here in the bookstore and she had no idea what to say to him. He looked even better than she remembered, and she had remembered him a lot. He had smelled delicious and her heart had beat a fast rhythm as he wrapped his around her. Maddy had honestly thought she was moving on, but one look at Sean, and she was back in fantasy land.

"Of course, we'll go. Right, Maddy?"

"Oh, um, yeah," Maddy answered, having no idea what she had just agreed to.

Sean looked her over. "You don't have other plans tonight? Hank said you've been pretty busy lately."

"No, I'm free tonight." She wouldn't admit out loud she hadn't made plans for tonight because she knew he was coming home and she didn't want to miss out if everyone got together.

"Good, then we can all get together and hang out like we used to."

Sean smiled and Maddy's knees went a little weak. Hanging out like they used to would be fun, but it would be even better if he realized she was a desirable woman whom everyone wanted and that he wanted her, too.

"Maddy?" Maddy turned at the sound of her name coming from behind her. It was Reid Mitchell, town veterinarian. *This is not happening.*

"Hi, Reid," she said.

"I'm sorry if I'm interrupting."

"Of course not. Fiona and I are just catching up with an old friend." She really wanted to tell him she was busy and to go away. "This is Sean Walker, Cassidy's brother. He's moving back to Hollow Moon." Maddy pointed from Sean to Reid. "Sean, this is Reid Mitchell. He's fairly new to Hollow Moon and is the town veterinarian." It reminded her of the scene from *Bridget Jones* when Bridget was learning how to properly introduce people at a party or social event.

The men shook hands, exchanged pleasantries, and then Reid turned back to Maddy. "I just wanted to ask you something, Maddy."

Maddy knew what was coming and if Sean hadn't been standing there, she would have been excited. Reid was handsome, had a great job, and was in her top three. "Yes, Reid?"

"I was wondering if you would go out with me next weekend," Reid asked.

"I would love to, Reid, but you know I'm dating several men and no one exclusively," Maddy said, trying hard not to look at Sean.

"I know, but I think we would have fun," he said, blushing.

"I would love to go out with you, Reid. How does next Friday night sound?"

"That's great. I'll call you to solidify our plans."

Reid leaned in, kissed her on the cheek, said goodbye to everyone, and left. Fiona and Maddy exchanged a look, but didn't say anything. It was the spell wrecking more havoc her life. If it had been at any other moment, Maddy would have been jumping up and down, excited that Reid had asked her out, but not today. Sean coming back to Hollow Moon, and the feelings he stirred up inside her just by standing in the bookstore, changed everything. Luckily, before she had to say anything else to Sean or Fiona, someone needed help with finding a book and she used it as an excuse to escape.

Chapter 7

Getting ready to hang out at the Blood Moon wasn't usually so stressful. It was Sean. He was actually here in Hollow Moon, so Maddy planned to look hot as hell and make sure he got a good look. She put on a short black skirt and a tight red tank top with her black heels. They were going to the Blood Moon Bar and there was sure to be plenty of dancing and playing pool, just like they had in high school, but this time with the added benefit of alcohol.

After pulling her hair up into a high pony tail, and adding some dramatic eye make-up and earrings, she was ready to go.

Fiona was ready first and waiting in the living room

when Maddy came downstairs. Fiona whistled and asked, "I'm guessing this is for Sean's benefit?"

Maddy wasn't even going to attempt to deny it. "Of course, just because I'm moving on doesn't mean I'm not going to stop trying to attract his attention. I'm still the same pathetic girl I was last week, just with a date every other night."

Fiona laughed. "That's my Maddy."

"By the way, who are you dressed up for? You look hot."

Fiona was wearing capri-length leggings with a lace pattern and a tunic top that was a little see-through with a camisole underneath. The outfit was sexy with a capital S. She was wearing her normally wavy chestnut hair straight and had played up her blue eyes with lots of eye make-up. "I'm not dressed up for anyone, I just knew you would be pulling out all the stops and didn't want to be left behind. Plus, you are a guy magnet, literally, and I might want some of your discards."

"You can have any of them, except for Hank or Reid. I still have dates with those two. I haven't really connected with anyone else and, luckily, the spell has broken easily with every man I've turned down."

"I'm still looking for a way to break it completely, but I haven't found anything yet."

"I know it sounds terrible to say I'm sick of being asked out, or that I don't want the attention, but when I was out with Declan, I had to turn down the valet, the waiter, and four others before we could eat dinner. It isn't easy to deal with. I don't think Declan noticed, but it was embarrassing when one guy left his pregnant wife to come ask me out."

"That does sound awful. The good news is I think you've turned down just about every man in Hollow Moon, so you shouldn't have to deal with too much while we're out tonight. And since you aren't on a date, it shouldn't be too bad if someone does come over. Plus, I saw how Sean reacted today when Reid Mitchell asked you out. He looked a little jealous so maybe seeing you out among your admirers will make him feel it even more."

Maddy wanted to believe Fiona, but she was trying to let go of her Sean obsession so she said, "I'm sure he was just irritated that Reid interrupted us to ask me out." She looked at her watch. "We'd better go. We don't want them to start the party without us."

The two cousins left in Fiona's car. Maddy took the time to calm herself so she could get ready to spend the night hanging out with Sean. She told herself repeatedly it wasn't any different than hanging out with Hank or any of their other friends. Of course, hanging out with Hank tonight would be different too since they were going out on a date Monday night. It was amazing how crazy her life had gotten since she had cast that damned spell.

Sean was already at the Blood Moon when Maddy and Fiona arrived. Hank had wanted to get there early to make sure they got one of the good pool tables and Sean couldn't argue with him. Plus, it was fun to just hang out for a while with his best friend, playing pool, and drinking beer. Now the girls were starting to arrive and the night would take a different turn. Maddy looked amazing and Sean wondered why he had never realized just how sexy she was.

Even the way she moved was incredibly sexy. He could almost imagine her moving toward him, completely undressed, except for those boots she had been wearing at the bookstore.

"She's pretty damn sexy," Hank said.

Sean nodded before he could stop himself. Then he shook his head and turned away from the two cousins who were walking his way. Maybe it was just being home that was making him think this way about Maddy. She was his friend, one of his best friends, and if they were to ever try to make it anything other than that, they would risk ruining what they had. She was one of the only people, besides his sister and Hank, that he really talked to and he wouldn't trade that for anything. Especially not for a romantic relationship that he was sure would eventually evolve into lies, yelling, and anger.

"Hi, guys."

But, oh, did even her voice do something to him.

He turned to face her. "Hi, Maddy. Hi, Fiona."

Everyone exchanged greetings and, just as they finished, Cassidy arrived.

"So, are we going to have a tournament?" Cassidy asked.

"Yeah, sounds like fun," Maddy added.

Hank and Fiona agreed, so they organized a roster. Fiona and Hank played first, while Cassidy got the first round of drinks, leaving Maddy and Sean to talk. If he was more suspicious, he might believe that there had been a plan to get the two of them together.

"Are you happy to be back, Sean?"

"So far. I went and saw the parents this afternoon, which is always such a joy. Then I went back to Hank's and did a search for some places to look at this week."

"Aren't there apartments available where Hank and Cassidy live?"

God, her lips were perfect. Whenever she spoke, all Sean could think about was her lips. What had she asked him? Something about apartments? "There are, but I don't want to live in an apartment. Since I will be working from home, I want an actual house with a yard and room to stretch out. I'm hoping I can find something in your part of town, actually."

"Usually, the houses near us don't go on the market. They are handed down to someone else in the family, like Fiona and me, but I think that the Jefferson's house is unofficially on the market. Mr. Jefferson passed away and his daughter lives in California. She doesn't want anyone to know she is selling, but I could call her for you and give her your number."

This was what small town life was like. "Is that the white house with the blue trim two doors away from yours?"

"Yes, I think it might need some work and it might be too big for just one person. I know Fiona and I complain about having too much house. Someday one of us will live there with a family, but for two single women it's a lot to keep up with."

Sean thought about seeing Maddy living in her house with a husband and children. It actually hurt, which was probably why he asked the incredibly stupid question before he could stop himself. "Would you ever think about renting out a room to a friend?"

Maddy froze and Sean wanted to kick himself. Of course, she didn't want him living in her house. Why would she? "Just ignore me."

"No, Sean. I think that actually might be a good idea. We don't use the third floor at all. It's more like an apartment with a small kitchenette and two rooms. I lived up there for a while when I was a teenager and went through a phase where I wanted to ignore Grandmother at all times. You could help us out around the house instead of paying rent. I know money isn't an issue for you, or at least it isn't, according to Cassidy, but it would be more helpful to us to have a handyman than a boarder."

Sean knew moving into the same house with Maddy would be a monumentally bad idea, but he couldn't help himself. "I don't know, Maddy. It sounds like I'm getting the better deal, but I'll take it if it is okay with Fiona."

At that moment the game between Fiona and Hank was over, with Hank the winner. Cassidy was next to play and she returned at just the right moment with their drinks. "If what's okay with Fiona?" she asked.

Fiona walked over and Maddy turned to her whispering quietly. When she turned around there was a big smile on her face. "Fiona thinks it a great idea."

"What does Fiona think a great idea?" Cassidy practically yelled.

Sean laughed. Cassidy had always hated not knowing something and it was great to see she hadn't changed in the time he had been gone. "Maddy and I were talking about me finding a place in town. We were talking about how the choices in town are either small apartments or extra-large houses. Then I asked if she and Fiona had ever thought about renting out a room in their house. A plan was hatched for me to rent the third floor. Instead of rent, I will be helping fix up some things around the house that need fixing."

He saw Maddy and Cassidy exchange a look, but couldn't tell what the look meant. "That sounds great, big brother. Plus, you can protect Maddy from all the crazy men she's been dating lately."

Hank frowned. "Hey, we aren't all crazy. Maddy doesn't need protected from me, do you Maddy?" He put his arms around her shoulders and looked at her longing-ly.

Maddy smiled at him, but it didn't quite reach her eyes. That was one thing Sean hadn't thought of when he had his great idea. He didn't want to see her date and come home with men. What if she brought home a man and he spent the night? What if Hank spent the night with Maddy?

"Hank, you need to play Cassidy," Sean said rather abruptly so Hank would have to get his arm off of Maddy. Everyone gave Sean an odd look.

Hank and Cassidy went to start playing their game and Fiona and Maddy grabbed their beers off of the tray that Cassidy had brought back from the bar. Sean sat down and thought about what was different about Maddy. He couldn't find a single thing, but while she was standing there two different men approached her and asked her out. She let both of them down gently and they walked away. They used to hang out like this during the summer while he was in college and she had never been approached by other guys. And from what he could gather, from talking to her, Cassidy, and Hank, during the last ten years she hadn't dated a lot.

She was one of the constants in his life. Always there if he needed to talk to someone. Now, she seemed to have this whole life he knew nothing about. Maybe that's why he felt this attraction. It was because he felt left behind. Sean shook his head. That sounded weak. He couldn't blame his attraction on feeling left behind, or because he was seeing her differently. The truth was he had started thinking differently about her before coming back to Hollow Moon and the feelings had only intensified since seeing her again.

Hank beat Cassidy and Maddy went next. Sean found himself cheering rather loudly for Maddy and trying to distract Hank when it was his turn. Maddy won and Sean got to play her for the championship.

Hank, Fiona, and Cassidy all declared that they were on Maddy's side and cheered loudly every time she knocked a ball in, which thanks to the distraction she provided in that short skirt and tight tank top, was a lot more often that Sean did. Maddy was the champion.

"So, what do I win?"

"Our admiration?" Fiona said.

"Another beer," Was Hank's suggestion.

"A dance?" Sean asked.

Maddy turned and looked at him. It was the first time that he'd felt that maybe she felt something for him other than friendship. The look in her eyes was full of heat and desire.

They stared at each other for a few moments before she nodded and walked toward him. He grabbed her hand and they walked to the dance floor.

Chapter 8

Sean woke up late and, after getting ready, he headed to Crescent Coffee. For someone who made his living selling coffee, it was odd that Hank didn't have any in his apartment. Sean took his laptop, so he could at least pretend to get some work done, but his mind was on what had happened between him and Maddy the night before. They had only shared that one dance, but it had been more than enough to change everything for him.

Now Sean had to decide if he was going to do something about this attraction or if he was going to work hard to ignore it. He still thought that acting on it was a bad idea.

He didn't want to mess up their friendship, but he wasn't sure that he would be able to ignore just how much he was attracted to her now.

Cassidy was behind the counter when he walked into the coffee shop. She waved and started on his coffee. That would be another perk of being home. In Boston he had to wait in long lines and no one remembered his coffee order. He picked a table in front of the window, so he could people watch, and near an outlet, because he planned on being there for a long time. Cassidy brought his coffee over, along with a chocolate pastry, and gave him a quick kiss on the cheek.

"When is your break?"

"I'm off in thirty minutes. I don't usually work on Sunday mornings, but Hank asked me to come in to cover for the normal person. I'm going straight home and back to bed as soon as my shift is over. Why are you up and about so early?"

"Hank doesn't have coffee in his apartment."

"Oh, I forgot about that. He comes to my apartment whenever he wants a cup and he isn't working."

"Really?" Sean asked suspiciously. He still thought that Hank had a thing for his sister, date with Maddy notwithstanding.

"Yes, big brother. He even has a key to my apartment in case something happens. You know that I am a grown up, right? Men do come to my apartment, maybe not as often as I would like them to, but they do."

"Okay, Cassidy. That's enough. I don't need to hear about you and men coming to your apartment."

Cassidy laughed. "I'll spare you the details. When are you moving into Maddy and Fiona's?"

That was a very good question, and one he didn't have an answer for at the moment. "I'm not sure. The bookstore is closed today, so I thought I would go over this afternoon and see what needs to be done in order to make the rooms move in ready. Maddy said that it used to be her apartment when she was a teenager, so it hasn't been used in a while. I'm sure it at least needs a good cleaning. Hopefully, before the week is out I'll be ready to move my stuff up here."

"So, you aren't regretting coming home?" Cassidy asked cautiously.

"No, in fact, I think I should have come home sooner. I just think I had something to prove. That I could make something of myself on my own. Plus, it was nice to get away from the folks. Not having to visit them and listen to them argue and fight with each other. I was there for not even five minutes yesterday before they started in on each other. I don't know how you've managed to stay in the same town as them this whole time, especially a town as small as Hollow Moon."

"Well, I don't really see them that much. They keep to themselves and we don't hang out at the same types of places. I think Maddy sees them more, but she said that they don't argue in public. I only visit on holidays and birthdays—dates when I can't get out of it."

"Cassidy, can I ask you a serious question?"

"Of course, you can, Sean." Cassidy sat at his table.

They had been talking for several minutes, but Hank hadn't called her back to work and no one had asked her for anything. It would seem that the coffee shop wasn't very busy on Sunday mornings in Hollow Moon.

"Do you think all relationships end up like Mom and Dad, eventually?"

He was afraid of how she was going to answer. He wasn't sure if he wanted her to confirm his belief or say that she believed that couples could have a happily ever after with hearts and rainbows.

"Sean, I'm not sure. I don't think that they do. I remember Grandma and Grandpa and they seemed to still truly be in love even after lots of years of marriage. I want to believe that couples can be happy after being together for a long time. I wouldn't want to be in a marriage like our parents and I hope to find someone who can put up with me someday."

"I've always thought that relationships were all like Mom and Dad's, but I'm thinking that maybe that was just my fear letting me use that as an excuse. I don't know."

"Is there any reason in particular that you are asking

about relationships? Is there some girl in Boston I need to know about?"

"No, there is no girl in Boston."

"But you didn't say there wasn't a girl here. Huh, who could it be?"

"Come on, Cass. I've only been home one day. How could I already have met someone in one day?" Sean knew he should have never brought up the topic. Cassidy wasn't going to let this go until she knew every detail.

"Unless—" She paused with her finger up to her chin as if in deep thought. "—it was someone you already knew and you were just rekindling a romance or starting one with someone you have known forever."

Rekindling? "Who would I be rekindling a romance with?"

"One of your many ex-girlfriends who live in town. I saw you dance with several of them last night. But I don't think that's who it is. I think it is a certain friend, who you plan on living with, that has you thinking about the R word."

Sean tried to play dumb. "Fiona? I don't have a thing for Fiona Simpson. She's beautiful and funny, but I've always thought of her as a little sister."

Cassidy slapped him on the shoulder. "Not Fiona. Maddy. I saw the way the two of you were looking at each other last night. And I have always thought your feelings for her were a little more than just friendship.

You are always more interested in what she's doing than anyone else. I don't think you realized it, but I did."

"Maybe it is Maddy, but I'm speaking in general terms. I haven't ever had a relationship that lasted more than a couple months because as soon as that first rush of getting to know you wore off I moved on. I didn't want to get to the arguing phase. I couldn't date someone I was actually friends with—it would ruin our friendship and that's not something I'm willing to do."

Sean was trying to think of a way out of their conversation when his phone rang and Hank called Cassidy over.

But before she walked away she said, "This conversation isn't over. I don't think it would ruin your friendship if you and Maddy dated. In fact, I think being friends before anything romantic happened might be the key to a great love story."

Sean looked at his phone and found Maddy's name on the caller ID. "Hello, Maddy."

"Hey, Sean. I wasn't sure if you would be up and around yet, but I thought I would risk it."

"I'm at Crescent Coffee actually. I was planning on letting you and Fiona sleep in and then call you to see what needs to be done to make those rooms we talked about move-in ready."

"That's why I called you too. I looked up there this morning and it isn't as bad as I thought it would be.

There were a few boxes that Fiona and I already moved to the attic and now it just needs a really thorough cleaning and new paint on the walls. I would say that you should be able to move in by next weekend."

"That's great. I can fly back to Boston, pack up what I'm bringing down here, and leave the rest for the movers. I actually don't have a lot to move. What time do you want me there to start cleaning?"

There was silence on the other end. "Oh, um, I thought Fiona and I would handle it."

"Instead of paying rent, I'm helping with things around the house. I think cleaning and painting the rooms I'm going to inhabit count as helping with things around the house, Maddy."

"You're right, Sean. I just wasn't thinking. You can come over whenever you want to. I think we are going to start soon and work on it all day today since the store is closed and neither of us had any other plans."

Sean almost asked if that meant she didn't have a date that night, but he stopped himself. He would go over there, help, and find out that way.

Plus, it didn't matter if she did have a date since he hadn't made up his mind about what he wanted. "Okay, want me to bring you anything from Crescent Coffee when I come?"

"Oh, yes!" she answered rather enthusiastically. "I would love a venti mocha and an apple fritter. I get used to having those every morning and, on Sunday, I go through a bit of withdrawal."

"Well, we don't want you to have to suffer while you are cleaning and painting. I might even bring an extra fritter as a sort of hazard pay."

"Oh, you are a great friend, Sean Walker. I gotta go. See ya later."

Sean hung up and sighed. Friend. Well, if that didn't settle everything. No matter what he was feeling for Maddy, she thought of him as a friend.

Chapter 9

Monday night Maddy was dressed for her date with Hank, but her heart wasn't in it. Now that Sean was back, this dating adventure had lost all its appeal. She really just wanted him and, even though she was going through with her date with Hank and her date with Reid on Friday night, she had politely said no to everyone else. By her, probably overestimated, calculations she had turned down ninety percent of the men in Hollow Moon and the others she had no contact with.

Luckily, Hank wanted to make her dinner at his house so she didn't have to worry about running into any men affected by the spell while out on her date tonight.

She had spent the day at the store and then come home to find a note from Sean, saying he was coming over the next day to finish cleaning before flying back to Boston on Wednesday to pack up and move his stuff. By the weekend, she would be living with the man she wanted more than any other and couldn't have.

Cassidy had confided in her that Sean was convinced all relationships ended up like his parents' and that was why he had never seriously dated. It made sense on some levels, but Maddy knew that if he really thought about it, he would realize how foolish it was to think that a couple who was truly in love couldn't stay that way forever.

A knock at the door pulled Maddy away from her thoughts. She walked from the living room to the entry way and opened the door. Hank stood there looking great. He was very tall with dark brown hair and gray eyes. His scruffy beard, probably from shaving when he got up to open the Crescent and not again before their date, gave him a bad boy vibe even though Maddy knew he was the opposite. "Hi, Maddy."

"Hi, Hank. Wanna come in or do we need to head to your house?"

"We better head straight to my place. I have chicken marinating and other things going that I don't want to leave for long." He held out her coat as she slipped it on and then grabbed her hand as they walked out to the car.

There was a spark between them, but it wouldn't be

fair to let this play out beyond tonight. Maddy had even thought about canceling, but didn't because she needed a break from her own house and the Sean invasion. She was ashamed of herself, but she was using Hank as a distraction.

"I could have driven myself over."

In fact, Maddy would have preferred it. At the end of the date, Maddy would tell him that she didn't want to see him like this again but she wasn't sure how it would go. No one had reacted badly so far, but she didn't really want a tense ride home.

"That's okay. I wanted to pick you up. Plus, it gave Sean time to clear out and head over to Cassidy's for a while."

Oh, crap. She hadn't even thought about the fact that Sean was staying with Hank until he could move into her house. Now he was leaving for a few hours so that she could have a date with his best friend? Well, that was one way to get a guy's attention, although not a good way. What if he decided to come back before the date was over? Or what if he didn't come back because he thought she would be spending the night? So many things about this night were wrong. Maddy should have canceled the date when Sean came back and she realized she wasn't over him.

"I forgot he was staying with you."

"Well, he's been spending a lot of time with you."

"We've almost got everything cleaned and ready for him to move in. Fiona has a list two pages long of things for him to work on to earn his rooms. She's the most excited about him moving in. She's always wanted her own personal handy man. He said that he's flying back to Boston on Wednesday and will be back by Sunday. He sure does move fast."

"That's the way he is. When there's something he wants, he goes after it."

Maddy didn't talk after that. She was too busy thinking about Sean going after what he wanted. She had a whole fantasy playing out in her head, of him coming home from Boston, realizing that in the short time they had been together, cleaning his rooms, that he couldn't live without her. He had been paying more attention to her since he had come back and she had attributed it to the spell. She reasoned he was less affected because of distance.

At least that was what she was telling herself. She didn't want it to be that he was so turned off by her that even a spell that made men fall in love with her didn't work on him. But the more she thought about it, the more she realized that he was acting different from the way he had in the past. Their conversations always had a flirtatious undercurrent and when he asked her to do something, she always answered yes. Maybe he was under the spell, but he just hadn't asked her out yet.

They pulled in to the apartments where Hank and Cassidy both lived. Sean would be two doors down during her date with Hank. Great. She walked up the stairs behind Hank, hoping that Sean would be at Cassidy's apartment and that Cassidy would keep him there, but Maddy wasn't that lucky. As they walked down the hall, Cassidy's door opened and Sean stuck his head out. "Hey, Mads."

Mads? That was new. "Hey, Sean. Sorry Hank kicked you out. I forgot you were staying with him or I would have suggested dinner at my place."

Sean frowned. "It's okay. I don't mind hanging out with Cassidy for an hour or two."

An hour or two. Was that Sean's way of hoping the date didn't go well or a warning that he wasn't going to stay away for long, no matter what?

Hank had heard what he said and turned back from his door. "An hour or two? We'll need more time than that, won't we, Maddy?"

Maddy felt everything freeze. She waiting for someone to speak and realized it wasn't that it *felt* like everything had frozen. Everything but her was actually *frozen*. Hank stood looking at her with a smile on his face, and Sean stood leaning on Cassidy's door frame, staring at her intently. How the hell had she done this? Maddy knew this was some witchy thing and pulled out her phone hitting Fiona's name in her contacts.

"Maddy?" Fiona asked when she answered.

"Fiona, I've frozen Sean and Hank in the hallway of the Moonbeam apartments."

Maddy looked around her. She had no idea if she had frozen everyone in the building or if someone was going to come out and find her with the two men.

"What?"

"I. Froze. Sean and Hank."

"I heard you, but I didn't think you could really mean froze, like as in they aren't moving. Is that what you mean?"

"Yes, that's what I mean. They were talking about how long our date was going to be. Sean said he would come back to the apartment in an hour or two and Hank said it would be a longer date than that. Then he turned to me and asked me. I didn't know how to answer and then they froze. Plus, Sean called me Mads. He's never called me anything but Maddy the entire time we've been friends. Why would he give me a nickname now?" Maddy heard Fiona laughing, which she did not appreciate.

"Maddy, darling, you have to calm down. Take a deep breath. I'm sure you somehow did this with your mind. Maybe casting the first spell opened up some sort of power channel within you and now whatever talents you possess are coming out?"

"Why are all of your sentences sounding like questions instead of statements?"

"Because I have no idea what's going on with you. Why don't you relax and imagine them unfreezing and see if that works, but don't do it until we hang up. If it works, text me when you get to Hank's, and if it doesn't, call me back. I'll pull out the family books and read to see if I can figure out what might be happening. You enjoy your night."

Maddy disconnected the call, took a deep breath, and imagined Sean and Hank unfreezing and talking to her. Instantaneously, they were both reanimated and waiting on her to answer the question about how long the date was going to last.

"Um, I don't know how long we will need tonight. I guess it depends on how good a cook Hank is."

Both men laughed, although she could tell that Sean's laughter was forced. Then Maddy followed Hank the rest of the way to his apartment. She kind of hoped that Sean would come rescue her after a couple of hours.

The date went well for the first two hours—Hank cooked a delicious meal of teriyaki chicken, rice, and steamed broccoli. They ate and talked. Maddy did have a lot in common with Hank, which she had known since they had been friends for a long time. Then they had moved to his living room and things had started to get awkward. Hank was sitting closer to Maddy than she would have liked, and he kept finding ways to touch her. Maddy knew she was going to have to find a way to tell him that she just didn't want this to go any further, when he started to do the "I'm going to kiss you" lean in. At that exact moment, there was a rattle at the front door and Sean came into the room.

Maddy jumped off of the couch, feeling like she had been caught about to cheat, which was ridiculous. Her whole life had become ridiculous. "Hank, I'm sorry. I just can't do this. I really do like you, but just as a friend. I'm sorry that I may have made you believe differently."

Hank blinked. He had that look that Maddy had become accustomed, too. The no longer under a spell look. "Um, it's okay, Maddy. I understand."

It was more than Maddy could take. Hank didn't really want to kiss her. None of the men she had gone out with really wanted to kiss her, and the one man she did want to kiss had just witnessed an embarrassing scene. Maddy could feel the tears starting to fall. "Sean, is Cassidy home?"

Sean nodded.

Maddy walked past both men and out the door of Hank's apartment. She could hear Sean calling for her, but she wasn't about to turn around and talk to him. She was upset and seconds away from an ugly cry. Maddy knocked on Cassidy's door and waited for it to open. Cassidy looked shocked to see her, but opened the door wider and shut it before Sean, who was storming down the hall, could make it to the door.

"Maddy, are you okay?"

Maddy nodded, sat down on Cassidy's couch, and then shook her head. She was so not okay. She could hear Sean banging on the door. "Tell Sean I'm fine and will talk to him tomorrow. I'll call Fiona to come pick me up." Maddy reached down beside her and realized she had left her purse and coat at Hank's. This made her cry harder. "Cassidy?"

Cassidy hadn't made it to the door yet, so she stopped and turned around.

"Can I use your phone and could you please get my things from Hank's apartment?" Maddy asked.

"Of course, you can use my phone, sweetheart. I will go get your stuff and be right back."

Cassidy left and Maddy took a second to regroup before calling her cousin. She had no reason to be this upset. She had brought the whole thing on herself.

The door to Cassidy's apartment opened and shut again. "You didn't have to go that fast, Cassidy."

"It's not Cassidy, Maddy." It was Sean.

"Sean, I'm fine and I don't want to talk." She picked up Cassidy's phone, but Sean took it from her hand and hung it back up.

"You aren't fine, and I'll do the talking if you don't want to. I'm sorry if I ruined your date."

Maddy looked up at Sean in surprise. He thought he was the reason she was upset. She could see it in his eyes.

He thought that he had upset her by coming in when
Hank was about to kiss her. "Sean, you didn't ruin the
date. I shouldn't have been out with Hank in the first
place. I knew that it was a bad idea before tonight, but
I'm trying like everyone wants me to, and it isn't going
well."

"Trying?"

"Trying to date. Trying to move on." God, Maddy
didn't know why she was holding anything back from
him. She might as well tell the truth. It would make her
feel better right now, even if she would hate herself for
doing it in the morning. "I'm trying to get over you, Sean.
I've had a crush on you for as long as I can remember
and everyone was telling me that I had no chance. That I
had to move on. Well, here I am trying and it sucks. It
sucks because you came home as soon as I decided I was
going to be strong and move on. Do you know how hard
it is to move on when I have to look at your face? And
what am I even moving on from? A crush that was always one sided. One you never knew about, and something that never would have mattered because you
weren't going to reciprocate any time soon."

Maddy wanted to stop talking, but she couldn't seem
to. Now that she was getting it out, it just seemed to keep
coming. "All those times you called to talk to me about
major decisions, I would tell myself that I was important

to you and that you just didn't realize it. It's pathetic, I know."

"Shut up."

She couldn't believe he would say that to her. "What?"

"I said shut up."

"I'm sorry. I know I shouldn't have told you all of this, and I understand if you don't want to move in to the house now. I understand if you don't ever want to—"

Maddy didn't get any farther. Sean pulled her into his arms, lowered his mouth to hers, and gently kissed her. It was a kiss she had dreamed about since she was fifteen.

Her fantasy Sean had never kissed her like this. The kiss began sweetly, but soon turned into something much more passionate as they enjoyed this first taste of each other.

Maddy didn't know if this was a kiss that would be repeated, but she wasn't going to take this one for granted, in case this was the only taste she ever got of the man she would probably love her whole life.

Chapter 10

The night ended with Sean taking Maddy home, kissing her a few more times, and then returning to Hank's apartment. Hank had been asleep, so Sean hadn't told him about kissing the woman he had just been on a date with.

Sean didn't look forward to talking about it with him. There was Cassidy, who had walked in right after the kiss and had known that something was up between him and Maddy. Then there was Maddy herself. Sean had no idea how she was going to be feeling today about what had transpired between them last night, but he was supposed to go over to her house at one o'clock to finish getting his rooms ready.

He was still planning on moving in, now more than ever, and he would see, then, if she wanted to forget what had happened or go for an encore. Sean was voting for the latter.

Luckily for Sean, Hank had already left for work so he didn't have to worry about facing him first thing this morning. And Cassidy had probably already left too, since she usually worked the early shift. Having friends with early morning jobs didn't usually make a difference to him one way or the either, but today he was happy for it. Sean had decided to fly out this evening instead of waiting till Wednesday, so he called the airline to change his ticket and got a flight for eleven that night. He had originally asked Hank to take him to the airport, but now he planned to ask Maddy to take him. That would give them some one on one time to talk. Sean packed his bag and took it to his car.

He went to Crescent Coffee and ordered his normal coffee. Hank pulled him aside and said, "No harm about last night. I don't know what I was thinking asking Maddy out, but it never would have worked. We've been friends for too long."

Sean didn't know what to say to that. He agreed that Hank and Maddy wouldn't have worked, but he also worried that the same could be said for him and Maddy. They had been friends for a long time and maybe that would be a problem. What if their relationship didn't work and they could no longer get along as they always had? "Hank, I have to tell you something about last night."

They sat down at what had become Sean's normal table in the short time he had been back in Hollow Moon.

Hank smiled at Sean. "What is it?"

"Last night, when Maddy left and she was so upset, I followed her."

"Yeah, I knew that. Cassidy said she passed you when she came to the apartment to get Maddy's stuff."

"Well, we talked about why she was upset and one thing led to another. We ended up kissing."

"Really? You and Maddy?"

"Yes. I didn't intend for it to happen, but it did."

Sean waited for Hank to react. He wasn't sure if his friend was going to punch him or just yell, but he didn't expect Hank to smile. "Finally. I wondered if you were ever going to make your move on Maddy. You've had a thing for her for a long time. Why haven't you done anything about it before now?"

"Wait. You don't care that I kissed the woman that you were on a date with last night?"

"No. I wouldn't recommend you do it again or with anyone else's date, but we are cool."

"Good. And I haven't had a thing for her for a long time. We've always just been friends. In fact, I'm not sure what we are now, but I know we are something other than just friends."

"I have to go back to work, but I'm sure Cassidy wants to know what's going on with you. She was freaked out this morning and wanted to know what I knew about you and Maddy. I'll send her over so she can bother you for a while. That will be your punishment for kissing my date."

Sean laughed. At least he knew that everything was going to be okay between him and Hank. Cassidy brought his coffee and a cinnamon roll. She sat down and stared at him. He stared back and wondered how long she would hold out before talking. It was a game he had played with her since she was a kid. Cassidy only made it two minutes before she started in on him. "So, I come back to my apartment and you have your arms around one of my best friends. She's been crying, but doesn't look upset. She looks more like she's been thoroughly kissed. Then the two of you leave. I get a cryptic text from her saying everything is wonderful an hour later and then nothing else the rest of the night. Tell me what is going on, big brother."

"Cassidy, all you need to know is that Maddy was upset and I thought it was because I had messed up her date. It wasn't because of that and she told me the reason she was upset. We talked and I took her home."

"And no kissing?" Cassidy asked slyly.

Sean thought about lying to his sister, but knew it was a bad idea. "There may have been a kiss or two."

"I knew it! I could tell you had kissed her when I came back in the apartment. So what does this mean?"

"I have no idea. I don't know if it was a one night thing, or if it could become something more."

"Well, I hope that it is something more. I've always thought that the two of you were meant for each other and you were just too blind to realize it."

"Thanks for the vote of confidence, sis." He took a drink from his coffee and looked around the shop. "Are you still planning on going to Full Moon on your break?"

"Yes, I always do. It's how Maddy gets her coffee. Do you want to take it to her?"

"No, I just wanted to ask you not to say anything to Maddy about me talking to you. I don't want her to think that I kiss and tell—or anything like that."

"I won't say anything to Maddy. But if she brings it up you better believe that we will be talking about you."

"I'm sure you will," Sean said with a smile. "I know how you guys can be about the gossip." Cassidy slapped his arm. "Oh, I'm leaving tonight for Boston. I want to get back as soon as possible, so I changed my ticket."

"Do you need me to drive you to the airport?"

"No, I'm going to ask Maddy."

"Oooo, so you can kiss her more?"

"Okay, that's enough talking to you. I'll see you when I get back from Boston."

They stood and hugged each other tightly. Sean

wasn't sure how he had made it so long without having Cassidy close. He had forgotten how great it was to be able to talk to her and see her all the time. They had never had the typical sibling rivalry because of the situation with their parents. It had always been Cassidy and Sean together growing up and it was nice to have that back now. "I need to go do a few things around town before I go to Maddy's this afternoon. I'll text you when I get to Boston."

"Okay, big brother."

❦❦❦

Maddy was trying to work, but her mind kept drifting to the night before. She had laid it all on the line for once and gotten the kiss of a lifetime. Now she had no idea what was going to happen between her and Sean. She would find out when he came to her house later today, but until then she was going to obsess over the kiss and what it could mean.

She was straightening the romance novels, which she couldn't seem to stay away from this morning, when Cassidy came in with her morning mocha and pastry. Maddy had forgotten that she was going to have to face Cassidy this morning.

She wondered what Sean had told his sister, if anything, about what happened the night before and what she was supposed to tell her about it, or not tell her about it.

"Hey, Maddy. I bring caffeine." Cassidy handed her the steamy cup of coffee.

"Thank you, Goddess of the Coffee Shop."

They both laughed and she started to feel better about how she was going to interact with Cassidy.

"You're welcome. I'm sure after last night you could use the extra help."

So much for not talking about last night, huh. "Last night?"

"Well, I just meant that it was an emotional and long night for you."

Maddy could tell by the blush spreading across Cassidy's face that that wasn't the only thing she was talking about. Sean must have mentioned to her what happened when they were alone in her apartment or when he had taken her home.

She wanted to be mad, but Cassidy was his sister and they were close. She didn't fault him with talking to her about what had happened. If anything, she felt bad that Cassidy was trapped between allegiance to her brother and a friend. "Cassidy, did Sean tell you what happened last night?"

Cassidy sighed. "He told me you talked and I guessed that you kissed. He just never confirmed if I was right—exactly. But I totally know that you did. I could tell when I came back into my apartment. You looked like you had just experienced the most amazing kiss ever."

Maddy looked around to make sure that no one was paying attention to her and Cassidy. Thank goodness, Miss May and Miss Aggie hadn't made it in yet. "Okay, yes we kissed—a couple of times. I was upset. He came in and I lost it. I told him how I felt about him and about everyone telling me how I had to move on and that was why I was going on a date with Hank. When I started saying that it was ridiculous for me to even think about him that way, he told me to shut up."

"He did not!"

"He did. And when I started spouting off more about how I was sorry about this and that, he stopped me from talking more by kissing me."

"Whoa."

"Yeah."

"Was it everything you had dreamed about?"

Maddy sighed. "It was everything I had dreamed about and much more. At first, I was worried that he had just kissed me to shut me up, but after he took me home we talked in the car and before I went inside, he kissed me again."

"So what does this mean?"

"I don't know. Did he say anything to you about that?"

"No, but he did say that he was going to your house

to finish up the rooms this afternoon and he's going to ask you to take him to the airport tonight."

"Tonight?"

"Oh, yeah, he's changed his flight to tonight so that he can get things done quicker in Boston. I'm thinking he wants to get back fast for some reason."

Maddy smiled, thinking that maybe she was the reason he wanted to get back so quickly. She hoped that she was the reason, anyway.

"I have to get back to work. Have fun this afternoon with my brother, but don't do anything I wouldn't do." Cassidy gave Maddy a hug and whispered in to her ear, "I'm so happy for you."

ℓℓℓ

Sean pulled up to Maddy's house and tried to calm the butterflies in his stomach. It was so dumb to have nerves. He knew how she felt. It was no longer a question of how she felt and if she liked him in return, but now he wondered what he was going to do about their kissing. Obviously the kiss had been the start of something, something great if the kiss had been anything to go by, but what exactly, Sean wasn't sure.

He got out of his car and walked up to the house. Maybe he should have brought flowers or something, but then this would have felt like a date to clean her house which was dumb. Although kissing while cleaning the rooms sounded like a great idea.

Maddy opened the door and they stood staring at each other for a few moments.

"Hey," she said, breaking the silence.

"Hi," he said back, unsure what to say next.

"Come in, we need to talk," Maddy said and Sean felt his hopes of kissing while finishing up his rooms evaporate.

She led him into the family room and sat next to him on the sofa. At least they weren't sitting on opposite sides of the room. "So, Maddy."

"Sean, I wanted to apologize again for unloading on you last night the way I did. I don't think it was fair to just dump my feelings on you without any regard to the position I was putting you in. I'm not sure if the kisses we shared were real, or if they were because you pitied me, but I want you to know that I understand if you want nothing more to happen between us."

He stopped her there. "I didn't kiss you because I pitied you. I kissed you because I had thought of nothing but kissing you since I came home and saw you at the bookstore. No, that's wrong. I thought about it before seeing you, but hadn't really let myself admit that I was thinking about you in that way. Maddy, I don't want to stop kissing you. In fact, I was trying to think of ways to fit kissing you in to finishing the work here at the house."

"Really?"

Sean moved close enough to Maddy that he could put his hands on either side of her face. "Can I kiss you, Mads?"

"Yes, Sean, I really wish you would."

They spent the next hour making out like teenagers on the couch in Maddy's family room. Then they went up to the rooms that would be Sean's by the end of the week and made out some more. When it was time for her to drive him to the airport not much had been done in the way of cleaning and they were both feeling a little sexually frustrated from all of the kissing.

"Do you think we are going to be okay? With you living here I mean? I know it's kind of like you are in your own apartment, but we will still be so close."

He grabbed her around the waist. "We will be fine. I think it will be wonderful to be together so much."

Maddy wasn't as sure as Sean seemed to be, but as she drove him to the airport, she admitted to herself that she did like the idea of being able to talk to him whenever she wanted, and kiss him as much as possible. The only problem she saw with their being together so much as they got used to being something more than friends was that it could be too much of a good thing in the beginning.

Plus, there were a few awkward things she had to deal with. Like the spell and the men who kept asking her out...and her date with Reid. She had almost forgotten about it, but right before they had left her house she had gotten a text from Reid with a reminder about that date for Friday night.

Now, she wanted to cancel, but she didn't know if that was fair. She needed to get Sean's opinion.

"Sean, there's something I want to talk to you about before you leave."

"Okay, we have about forty minutes before we get to the airport, so let's talk."

"I have a date Friday night." Silence. Maddy looked over at Sean. "Are you going to say something?"

"What do you want me to say?"

"I'm not really sure." And she wasn't sure. She didn't know how she wanted him to respond. She didn't want him to tell her she couldn't go out with Reid, but she didn't want him to not care either.

"I can't tell you not to go, but I will say that I don't like the idea of you going out with someone else. I don't like the idea of another man getting to sit across from you and listen to you laugh. I will understand if you want to honor your commitment, but I won't like it at all."

Maddy smiled. She hadn't known what she wanted him to say, but he had said the right thing. "I'll cancel the date. I didn't really want to go, just like I didn't really want to go out with Hank. I just feel bad canceling."

"I know you do. I will try to be back by Saturday and

then we can go out on a real date," Sean said as he leaned over and gave her a kiss on the cheek.

Maddy smiled. It seemed as if everything she had wanted was starting to come true. Now all she had to do was find a way to reverse the Make Me a Match spell and cancel her date with Reid.

Chapter 11

The chorus of "I'm Sexy and I Know It" was blaring from Maddy's phone the next morning at the ungodly hour of six am, waking her up and making her hate the world and everyone in it. Who called someone at six in the morning?

Maddy thought about ignoring it, but since the only phone calls that came that early were calls where something was wrong she answered.

"'Lo?"

"Hello?"

Maddy sat up and smoothed her hair as if the person on the other end of the phone could see her. "Sean?"

"I'm sorry I called so early. I forgot about the time

difference and then I had dialed and couldn't wait to talk to you."

Maddy smiled. "That's okay. I miss you, too. How was your flight?"

"Fine. My apartment seems rather cold and empty though. I got used to having Hank or Cassidy around constantly."

"And when you get back you will always have Fiona or me underfoot."

"I don't see a problem with having you under me, Mads."

"You called me Mads again. Where is that coming from?"

He was quiet for a moment and Maddy felt bad for asking. "I don't know, Maddy. If you don't like it, I won't use it anymore. It just seems to fit you in my mind."

"Sean, I like it. You've just never given me a nickname until the night we kissed. It was one of the things I went a little crazy over than night. In the hallway before the date started, when you were messing with Hank, you called me Mads." *And I froze you, but we don't need to talk about that.* "What are your plans for today?"

"I'm boxing up everything I plan to bring with me to Hollow Moon and putting it in the moving van. I'm also going to box up the stuff I'm afraid the movers would break. The rest I'm going to let them pack up and move for me. What's the point in having the money if it isn't to get someone else to do the grunt work when it comes to moving?"

"Sounds like a good plan."

"I should be able to finish today and run the few errands I need to close bank accounts and transfer things to the ones I opened yesterday in Hollow Moon. I have everything in order so I should be able to hit the road tomorrow morning and, if I drive all day Thursday and Friday, I should get to Hollow Moon around ten o'clock Friday night."

"Wow. I didn't think you would be back so soon. I thought you would take a few days in Boston."

"That was my original plan, but now I just want to get back to you."

They talked for a few more minutes and then hung up. Maddy sighed. There was something off about how excited Sean was to talk to her and get back to Hollow Moon. Suddenly she sat up and yelled for Fiona.

Fiona came running into Maddy's room. She took in the tears streaming down Maddy's face and her shaking hands.

"What is it, Maddy!" she asked as she took a seat on the bed next to her cousin.

"It's Sean."

"Oh my gosh. Did something happen to him in Boston?"

"No, he's okay, but I think—" Maddy paused. "I think he's under the spell. I think that's the only reason he's with me."

Fiona took a deep breath. "Why would you think that?" she asked, although she had wondered the same thing herself. If he wasn't, she wondered why he hadn't been affected. The researcher in her wanted to study Sean's reaction, or lack of reaction to the spell, and find out what was happening.

"Well, he called me this morning and said that he was hurrying to get back. Originally he had planned to spend time in Boston and then come back to Hollow Moon. Now he's heading back first thing tomorrow."

"Okay, but don't you want him to hurry back fast?"

"Yes, but it was the way he said it. Like he was desperate to be back."

"I don't know. I didn't get the vibe that he was under the spell before you guys hooked up. He was hanging out with all of us the other night and, while there were some flirty vibes between the two of you, he didn't fall over himself to impress you or ask you out like the other guys have been."

"That's true. I didn't think he was either, but today it felt different."

Fiona laughed. "Well, Maddy, darling, crazy cousin of mine. That's because things are different. He has acknowledged that he has feelings for you and you have done the same. There are going to be some definite changes in your relationship with Sean."

Maddy groaned. She was being irrational and she knew it. She just didn't want this thing that was happening between her and Sean to be because of that stupid spell. She wanted it to be real. Real love or real lust. Whatever, just real. "You are probably right. I am just tired and not quite awake since I haven't had any coffee."

"I thought it was odd we were having this conversation without any magic elixir."

They both laughed. "Do you think, since I'm obviously Wendy Witch now, that I could learn a spell to make coffee on demand?"

"Wendy Witch?" Fiona shook her head. "I don't think there is a spell and, surely, that would be something I would have found in the book. That would be the first spell that most witches would want to learn."

"That and how to conjure up dates," Maddy said sarcastically.

"Well, of course," Fiona agreed.

"I guess I better get up, but you can cuddle in here if you don't want to go back to your bed. I have to go to an early morning breakfast with the Main Street Association before the store opens. Reid should be there, so I'm going to cancel our date then. There will be people around so I don't think he will get too upset and, since he only asked me out because of the spell, once I turn him down, the spell should break. It will be fine."

"Are you telling me or yourself?"

"Both."

Maddy got up and got ready for her meeting. She knew that everything was going to be okay, but there was a part of her that worried about telling Reid that their date was off. She thought he was someone who might have asked her out without the aid of the Make Me a Match spell, and she had no idea if that made a difference in how someone was affected by it—especially since she had messed up when she cast it.

Chapter 12

Her morning meeting had been long and boring, as usual, and Maddy was so grateful to be back in her office at the bookstore. The Main Street Association was the only part of owning Full Moon Books that she didn't love.

As the youngest member, they always singled her out to head committees and lead projects, since she had lots of "time and energy." Today, they had voted for her to organize the Spring Fling Dance and Silent Auction that would take place in April. It would be fun, but a lot of work.

Maddy was lucky that she had Cassidy and Fiona, who loved to help her with the community stuff.

She had just sat down at her desk when her cell rang. "Hello."

"Hi, Maddy. I was calling to see how the association meeting went this morning."

It was Reid, who should have been at the meeting that morning. She had planned on canceling their date then, but he hadn't shown up.

It was a little creepy that he was calling just minutes after it ended. If he hadn't been able to make it, surely he would still be busy.

"It was okay. We talked about Spring Festival and I got suckered into planning the Spring Fling dance. Everyone missed you. Did you have an early morning appointment?"

Reid laughed. "Something like that."

"Um, Reid. I was wondering if we could meet for coffee today."

He didn't answer for a few moments and she wasn't sure if he was going to answer her or not. "I don't have anything scheduled around three this afternoon."

"That's about the time I usually leave the store. Do you want to meet at Crescent Coffee at three?"

"Okay. Is everything okay, Mads?"

Mads? Why would Reid call her that? The only person who had ever called her that was Sean and that was only recently. Everything about this phone call felt off to Maddy and she wanted to get off the phone with Reid as quickly as she could. "Everything is fine. I'll see you at three at Crescent."

She didn't wait for him to say anything else before she hung up the phone. She didn't really want to meet with him, but she wasn't sure that the Make Me a Match spell would be broken if she broke their date over the phone. Reid had seemed like a really nice guy before, but over the last week something had changed. Maddy wasn't sure if it was her, because of her relationship with Sean, or if it was something the spell was doing to Reid.

Maddy's phone rang again and she almost didn't want to even look at the caller ID to see who could be calling her in fear that it was Reid again. It wasn't. It was Sean. After they had hung up this morning, she didn't think she would hear from him again until tonight, but seeing his name on the caller ID was a pleasant surprise.

"Hello, Sean Walker."

"Hello, Maddy Simpson."

They both laughed and Maddy relaxed a little. She was probably being silly and overly sensitive about the Reid thing, projecting fears and worries onto him and his behaviors.

"Are you at work?"

"I just got in. Wednesdays are Main Street Association days, so I had an early morning meeting, and now I'm settling in to answer some emails and order some new books before we open."

"Sounds like fun."

"It is. What have you been doing since we talked at the crack of dawn?"

"I've packed up my bedroom and office. I'm about halfway done with the living room. The rest I'm leaving for the movers. However, I'm getting ready to leave to run some errands and have lunch with some friends from college, but I wanted to call and talk to you first."

Maddy smiled. She liked that he thought about her so much. She still feared that his feelings were in part because of the spell, but she wasn't going to dwell on that until she figured out a way to prove it one way or the other. "I'm glad you called. I had an odd conversation with Reid Mitchell just now and it made me feel off. Hearing your voice helps."

"Odd, how?"

She could hear the tension in his voice—a change from his casual tone of just seconds before. They had spent so many hours on the phone together that she could probably tell his moods just by the tone of his voice, even if his words were saying something different. "He just said things to me that don't sound right. I'm not sure how to explain it. He didn't come to the meeting this morning, but he knew exactly when it was over and when I was back in the store. Like he had been watching. Then he called me Mads." She felt silly for making such a big deal out of someone else using Sean's nickname for her, but it was something only he called her and she didn't like to hear it coming from someone else.

"He did what?"

"He called me Mads."

"But only I do that." Sean sounded upset that someone else had used his nickname for her and she loved it.

"I know and I don't know when he would have heard you call me that, either. You don't do it often and haven't been doing it for long. So unless he is watching me, he wouldn't have had an opportunity to overhear you use that nickname."

Sean took a deep breath that was audible through the phone. "Maddy, I'm gonna sound like a possessive asshole for a minute, but I don't want you seeing him at all. I know I told you that I wasn't going to tell you one way or the other about your date with him, because it was before you and I started whatever it is that we are, but he doesn't sound right. I want you safe and he doesn't sound safe. So please don't go out with him or be anywhere alone with him."

"I'm already planning on canceling the date. In fact, that's what I was talking to him on the phone about today. I'm meeting him at Crescent Coffee at three o'clock. Hank will be there and it's always busy that time of the day. I don't think Reid's dangerous, but he's off somehow. And I don't think you're a possessive asshole, either. I like that you want to protect me and keep me safe. I promise to be careful."

"Okay. I just don't like the way he's coming across, but I know that you can take care of yourself." He paused. "Shit. I have to go or I'm going to be late for lunch. Call me after you meet with him to let me know how it goes, okay?"

"I will, Sean. Have fun at lunch."

"Bye."

They hung up and Maddy sat in her office for a few minutes, just thinking about Sean. He trusted her to handle all of this on her own without some big strong man to help, but he still wanted to protect her in some way. It made her feel special that he had gotten so upset on her behalf.

Talking it out with Sean had made her realize just how much Reid had to be watching her or paying attention to what went on around her to know some of the things he knew. It made her want to crawl into her bed and not come back out, but she wasn't going to do that. Instead, she'd get done what she needed to do and then break the spell enchanting him at three o'clock.

As three o'clock came, she found herself at the Crescent with more than a few nerves. She'd called Hank earlier in the day to make sure that he was going to be there when she came in for her break-up date. Maddy knew that she'd feel better if he was there with her. Hank admitted that Sean had already called to make sure that he was going to be there, too. Instead of irritating her that Sean was being possessive, Maddy liked it.

Reid walked in and smiled at her. The butterflies that had been playing around in Maddy's stomach decided to go ballistic.

He looked so happy to see her, but she wasn't happy to see him. It felt wrong to even be meeting him for coffee, there was no way she could have gone on a date with him.

"Maddy, you look beautiful today," Reid said as he sat down beside her at the small table.

Maddy had already ordered her coffee. She waited for Reid to say something about ordering his, but all he did was stare at her.

"Thanks. Um, Reid, there was a reason I asked you here today."

"I thought it was probably because you wanted to get everything in order for our date on Friday night. Make plans and stuff. I was so happy you wanted to get together early."

"Actually it is about our date on Friday." She paused and took a deep breath. "Reid, I'm sorry, but I'm not going to be able to go with you on Friday night."

"Why not?" he yelled, his voice sounding less like the mild veterinarian she was used to and more like a WWF wrestler.

"I've started seeing someone else, and I think it could develop into something serious."

"Who is he?" he yelled again, this time getting up in her face.

Maddy turned and looked for Hank. She saw him making his way over to her table.

She thought that when she broke the date Reid would be okay with it. They would share a cup of coffee and that would be that. The spell was supposed to break when she turned him down, but as she looked at him across the table, she could see him getting visibly angrier as the seconds went by.

This wasn't what was supposed to happen. Of course, lately nothing was going the way she thought it would, so why was she surprised?

"Reid, you're yelling at me. It doesn't matter who I'm seeing. You knew that I was going on other dates when we made our date and that ours wasn't anything serious."

"I knew you had a couple of other dates, but I was sure that when we went out, you would know that we were meant to be together. You aren't even giving us a chance. Tell me who it is."

Hank came up to the table and sat down. "Reid, you need to quiet down. You are yelling at a lady, and that's not okay."

Maddy smiled. Hank was very calmly taking over

and she knew that he would be able to get Reid to stop freaking out—at least she hoped so.

Reid turned to face Hank. "Hank, I don't mean to be rude, but this has nothing to do with you." Reid looked between Maddy and Hank. "Unless you are the man she's seeing now and thinks she could be serious with."

Maddy hated that she was being talked about as if she wasn't even there. She wondered if she could leave and they would continue having the conversation without her. If she could, she would, but Reid was sure to notice if she got up from the table. Instead she said, "It isn't Hank and, like I said earlier, it doesn't matter who it is. The only thing that matters is that I'm canceling our date. I'm sorry and I hope we can still be nice to each other when we see each other in town like we always have." Maddy paused and murmured under her breath. "You aren't even supposed to care once I break the date." But it hadn't been said quite as low as she had thought and Reid heard her.

"Why wouldn't I care that you were breaking our date? Maddy, I really like you and have been looking forward to our date a lot. I think you owe it to me to tell me who you are going out with if that means you can't go out on a date with me. If it isn't Hank, and I know your date with Declan and Josh didn't go well, who else could it be? The only other man you have spent time with is Sean Walker, but he left town again. And everyone knows you've had a crush on him forever, and he never felt the same way about you."

How did he know so much about her? Reid hadn't gone to school with them and had only lived in Hollow Moon for a few years. He had moved to town several years after Sean had moved away, so there was no way that he had seen her crushing on Sean. Even though there was no truth to his statement about Sean never feeling anything for her—he did feel something for her now—it still hurt to know that people in town saw her as the pathetic girl in love with someone who wouldn't love her back.

Part of her wanted to run and hide away so that his words couldn't hurt her, but another part—the witchy, bitchy part—wanted to let him know that it was the sexy Sean who she was turning him down for. Guess which side of her won?

"Actually, Reid, it is Sean that I'm seeing. On Monday night he confessed that he had started having feelings for me and that he had never realized that I had feelings for him. As you said yourself, I've had a crush on him forever, so I'm sure you can understand why I would want to see where this thing with him could go."

Why wasn't the spell breaking?

Hank was holding out her coat, so Maddy got up, put it on, and started gathering her things. She guessed Hank didn't think she was going to be able to rationalize with

Reid and he was probably right. The spell didn't seem to be breaking and Reid didn't seem to be understanding that she didn't want to go out with him because there was someone else. Maddy really needed to talk to Fiona and see where she was on finding a spell to break the Make Me a Match spell. That might be the only way to deal with Reid.

"You're just going to leave?"

Reid started to grab her arm, but Hank stopped him. "Okay, that's enough. I'm going to take Maddy to her car and you're going to wait right here. We are going to have a talk about the proper way to behave around a woman, and let me tell you that one of those things is that you don't grab her if she is trying to leave," Hank said as he started walking Maddy out of the coffee shop. He whispered to Maddy, "Are you okay?"

"Yes, thank you. I really didn't think he would act that way. I just thought I would cancel the date, we would share a cup of coffee, and it would all be over."

Hank looked her over and Maddy felt a little uneasy. The spell had broken on Hank the night in his apartment, she was sure of it—at least she had been. "Maddy, any guy would be upset about being dumped by you."

"Dumped? We haven't even gone out on a date yet. You can't dump someone you haven't gone out with yet." Maddy unlocked the door to her car, but she didn't get in yet. She had to make sure that things were okay between her and Hank. "You aren't upset about how our date turned out, are you, Hank?"

He looked her in the eyes. "I will admit that I'm a little disappointed that it didn't go better, but I've always known that you and Sean were meant to be together. I had a feeling when he came back that my chances with you were over. I don't think we would have worked out as a couple, anyway. I just didn't think that our one date would have ended with you in tears and then kissing my best friend." He said all of that with a smile on his face, so Maddy knew that he wasn't upset about how things had ended and, hopefully, that meant that the spell didn't affect him anymore. She wondered if there was some connection between her and the man before the spell, if it had a different effect and what that meant for Reid and Sean.

"I didn't think it would end that way either, Hank. I never thought that anything would happen between Sean and me, but I'm so happy that you aren't upset with either of us."

Hank kissed her on the cheek. "Of course, I'm not upset. I'm happy for the two of you and hope that everything works out for you. I'll go deal with Reid. You go home and have a glass of wine."

Maddy thanked Hank for dealing with Reid and got into her car. She was ready for the day to be over and for Sean to come back to Hollow Moon.

Chapter 13

It was Friday night and Sean was coming back to Hollow Moon to stay. Like many Friday nights before, Maddy, Cassidy, and Fiona were drinking margaritas and talking about men. The only difference this Friday night was that, instead of talking about how to help Maddy to get over Sean, they were trying to figure out ways to get Maddy under Sean.

"So, what time is he supposed to be back?" Fiona asked.

"The last time I talked to him—"

"Which was like an hour ago," Cassidy interrupted.

Maddy threw the couch pillow at her. "Like I was saying. The last time I talked to him he was about two hours away, but he thought he might stop and eat some-where. So I'm not sure when he will get in, but it should be in the next few hours."

She was trying to act like she was calm about Sean finally getting back to Hollow Moon, however, she was anything but calm. She was nervous, excited, worried, and happy all at once. They had talked several times a day while he'd been driving from Boston and had a very naughty conversation the night before which had led to a very bad night's sleep. She was looking forward to being able to see him at the same time while talking to him to-night and maybe kissing him a little, too. Their conversa-tions over the last two days had covered everything she could ever imagined talking to him about. They had al-ways shared everything with each other, except talk about their romantic lives. Sean had talked to her about his par-ents, their dysfunctional relationship, and his fear about being in a relationship himself. Maddy now felt like she knew him even better than she had before.

"Maddy's thinking about Sean," Fiona said in a sing-song voice.

"How do you know?" Maddy asked.

"You are making the Sean face," Both Fiona and Cassidy said at the same time.

All three erupted into laughter.

"The Sean face?" Maddy asked as she took a big drink out of her second margarita.

"Your face takes on a dreamy quality and you wear a secretive smile. You look like you are thinking about kissing or something else that I don't really want to think about since we are talking about my big brother," Cassidy answered.

"Oh, really, because ten minutes ago the two of you were talking about Fiona spending the weekend with you so I could finally get some with your big brother."

"Well, that's true. I'm trying to be a good friend and sister here. I know that when he comes back, the two of you are probably going to want to be alone. At least you *should* want to be alone. So I was trying to be helpful. That doesn't mean I want to think about you and him kissing or anything else."

Maddy laughed. She could really give Cassidy a hard time and start talking about all sorts of naughty stuff she wanted to do with or to Sean, but she wasn't that mean or that drunk. Instead she said, "Thank you for being a good friend. I don't know that we are ready to take it to that level." *Please let him be ready to take it to that level.* "But it might be nice to be alone some this weekend. That doesn't mean I want to kick Fiona out of the house if she doesn't want to leave." Maddy looked at Fiona. Sean moving into the extra rooms upstairs had been one thing when she just had a crush on him. If they were a couple it might be too awkward for Fiona.

"I'm planning on having an epic sleepover with Cassidy. You're going to be jealous of how much fun we have and wish you were with us instead of a stinky boy. Plus, I want you and Sean to have some amazing sex. I don't have any problems with it. You can get it on in every room except mine and the kitchen, because we eat in there and that's gross. It's long overdue and I want it to happen almost as much as you do—almost." Fiona laughed. "Plus, I'm sure he'll be moving stuff in and around all weekend and if I'm at Cassidy's I won't have to help."

"So you want me to have sex with him and you don't want to help him move in."

"Pretty much." Fiona grabbed the pitcher of margaritas. "Who wants another?"

All three girls did and so Fiona poured them each another very large drink. Sean was going to find an intoxicated Maddy when he made it to Hollow Moon that night, and she thought that might be a lot of fun for both of them. She would be able to overcome her inhibitions and show him just how much she had missed him, but as she didn't want to get too drunk to enjoy the fact that he was home, this would be her last drink.

ℰᗝℰᗝ

Sean opened his door and got out of the car, but couldn't seem to move any farther. Maddy looked amazing, although even that wasn't a good enough description. Her hair was pulled up part of the way and looked sexily messy. Her dress looked like he could untie one bow and the whole thing would fall off. He really wanted to untie that bow.

"You're back," Maddy said as she walked toward him.

"Sure am. Are you glad?" he asked.

"Sure am," she echoed as she reached his car.

They stared at each other for a few seconds before the urge to touch her overwhelmed him. He pulled her to him by her hips and tilted his mouth over hers. The kiss was gentle at first and then the passion escalated. They stood there, in her driveway, making out for several minutes before he was able to make himself pull away.

"Welcome home," Maddy said, smiling.

"Thanks. I'm starting to think that I should have come home a lot sooner," he said.

"You made the drive in two days and the whole trip in four. I don't think you could have done it faster."

He pulled her close again. "I meant I should have come home to Hollow Moon sooner. I shouldn't have stayed gone for so long. I might have realized what was right in front of me if I had. I can't believe that I might have missed out on what we could have together."

Maddy grabbed his hand and started pulling him into the house. What was a guy to do but follow the sexy woman inside? She led him through the living room and up the stairs. His eyes never strayed far from her delectable ass, and the fact that he couldn't see any panty lines, had him looking really hard. She led him into her room and shut the door behind him.

"We're home alone."

"We are?"

"Yes."

Done talking, he took her into his arms, put his mouth on hers, and brought their bodies together. Sean didn't think there was anything better than the feel of her up against him, except maybe if they were both without the clothes that were still between them. She must have felt the same way because she pulled away and started removing his shirt.

"I think we need to take this off too, sweetheart," he said, pointing at her dress.

Maddy smiled at him and he felt his cock pulse against his jeans. If they weren't naked and together soon, he was going to embarrass himself. She grabbed the tie on the side of her dress and began to pull. Slowly the dress came undone, opened, and fell off her shoulders, leaving her dressed in a black push up bra and tiny thong. It was the sexiest set of lingerie he had ever seen.

"Your turn," she said, smiling at him.

His hands were shaking a bit as he undid the buttons on his jeans. Leaning over to take off his shoes, he didn't notice that Maddy had walked behind him until he felt her hands on his ass.

"What are you doing?" he said, while standing back up.

"I thought I would help you hurry up."

Working together, they quickly had him undressed. Sean couldn't wait anymore. He had to have her and hoped that she could forgive him for making this first time together fast and hard. He picked her up against him and carried her to the bed. "I have to have you now, Maddy. I can't wait."

"Then take me, Sean."

And he did.

Chapter 14

Maddy barely made it through work the next day, and it was all Sean Walker's fault. He had woken her up with coffee and breakfast in bed that morning, driven her to work after asking to use her car for some errands since his was still full of stuff, and then checked in several times during the day to make sure she was "having a good day," "did she need coffee?" "just to say hi." She was going mad with wanting to kiss his face.

Finally, Fiona and Annie had told her to go home and to take Sean with her. Annie had laughed and told her that if a man who looked like Sean had made her breakfast in bed, she wouldn't have come in to work at all. She would have come down with hot-guy-in-my-bed-itus and called in sick.

Fiona told her not to come to work until she had gotten everything out of her system.

Maddy called Sean. "I'm ready to leave for the day."

"Don't you usually work later?"

"Yes, and if you aren't done with what you were going to do, I can go hang out at Crescent Coffee for a while and read, but I'm being kicked out of my own store."

He laughed. "Kicked out?"

"Yes, you and I are driving Fiona crazy so she's making me leave. I don't mind, though. I wasn't getting much done."

"Why not?" Maddy could hear his smile through the phone.

"This really good-looking guy keeps showing up and checking on me. Plus, he made love to me last night, twice, and I just can't quite quit thinking about it."

"Well, I think I know what you should do."

"You do?"

"Yes, I think you should meet that guy at Crescent Coffee. He might be about thirty minutes, but he knows that you love to read and probably won't mind having to wait a few minutes for him."

"That sounds like an excellent plan. I will see him in about thirty minutes."

They hung up and Maddy grabbed her things. She walked back out to the front of the store where Fiona was shelving some books.

"I'm leaving. I called Sean and told him that I was being kicked out of my own store. He thought it was hilarious. I'm going to meet him at the Crescent in thirty minutes, but I thought I would get some reading done and go early. Are you staying with Cassidy again tonight?"

"Yes, because I'm really hoping that the two of you have wild monkey sex all over the place."

"Fiona Simpson, please don't say things like that in public." Maddy could feel herself blushing—not really because she was embarrassed, but because she was thinking about having wild monkey sex with Sean. It had been the best sex she had ever had, and she was more than okay with having a lot more.

"Have fun," Annie called as Maddy walked out of the bookstore.

I will, Maddy thought.

∞∞∞

Sean walked into Crescent Coffee and immediately saw that something was wrong with Maddy. She looked upset and her whole body language said to stay away. When they had last talked on the phone she had been fun and flirting with him, so he had no idea what could be wrong.

He sat down beside her, but she didn't seem to notice him. "Maddy, sweetheart, what's wrong?" Looking around he saw his sister and waved her over.

Maddy turned her head toward him as if just noticing he was there. Her face crumpled and tears started falling down her face. "Maddy, you're worrying me. Tell me what's wrong."

She pointed to something on the table. Sean picked it up and read it.

> *Maddy Simpson is nothing but a cock-tease and a whore. She leads men on with no intention of following through. If you've been led on by the whore join our group. Maddysawhore@yahoo.com*

There was information for where and when the group would meet and who was organizing it—Reid Mitchell the veterinarian who had asked Maddy out his first day in town. She had called off their date. Hank and Maddy had both told Sean there were problems when she canceled the date. Hank had thought that he had handled it, but obviously the guy was still upset. Maddy looked so hurt, Sean wanted to take her home and keep her there so things like this couldn't bother her at all.

Cassidy walked over with a glass of water for Maddy and took the note from Sean. Her face turned red as she read it and Sean knew that if Reid showed his face in the coffee shop anytime soon his sister would kick his ass.

"Maddy, I'm sorry you saw that. You and Hank both told me that the guy was upset when you canceled the date. I guess this is just how he is reacting. I know there is no one else in town, who would go to any type of group like this, and no one thinks you are a whore or a cock-tease." God, he hated even saying the words to her.

"Sean, I went on some dates, knowing that I didn't really like the guy and that I would never like him like I liked you. What does that make me? I know I'm not a whore. You have to sleep around to be a whore and I haven't had sex in forever, but I'm not sure that I couldn't be called a cock-tease."

She had told him that it had been several years since she had had sex before last night so there was no way anyone could call her a whore. He knew, as well as anyone, who really knew Maddy, that she wasn't a cock-tease.

"A cock-tease is someone who makes the guy think he's going to get lucky. Did you do that?"

Maddy shook her head and looked upset again. Sean slid the paper to his sister and pulled Maddy in for a hug. "We are going to ignore this, go home, and get ready for our date."

Maddy looked at him and he could see by her eyes

how upset she was. "Sean, can we stay in tonight? I saw at least ten of these around town on my way over here. I think he's putting them only in places where I would see them, but I still don't want to go out where others who have seen them might be. We could fix dinner ourselves and watch a movie."

Sean would do whatever she wanted. This flyer had really upset her. "Of course, we can do that as long as you will wear your flannel pajamas."

Cassidy glanced up from the note. "Flannel pajamas, huh. I would have thought you would like the lingerie she was wearing last night." She paused for a second and then turned to Maddy who had turned as red as a tomato. "Reid Mitchell is a piece of dirt. Hank said that we aren't to let him in here anymore and lots of people are upset for the way he treated you. This isn't going to reflect badly on you, but it will on him. No one will believe you are a whore or a cock-tease. It's ridiculous—when you went on, what? Four dates in a two-week span after not dating for a year and even longer before that? Everyone in town was happy for you that you were putting yourself out there and then, when it started circulating about you and Sean, I've had a lot of people tell me that they are glad my brother finally wised up."

"Sean? Can we go?" Maddy asked.

He stood and saw Reid Mitchell watching them through the mirror. He turned to tell Maddy he would be right back, but when he turned back around Reid was gone.

Sean and Maddy left the coffee shop and headed back to her house. He wanted to take her mind off of the flier and Reid, so he thought about what Cassidy had said when he had mentioned the flannel pajamas. "So what lingerie was Cassidy talking about and how does my sister know about your naughty underwear?"

Maddy looked at him and then laughed so loud that it looked like it had startled her. "Oh, my gosh. I needed that. I can't believe that you caught that in Cassidy's little speech."

"Sorry, I hear 'lingerie' in relation to you and it is going to stick in my head."

"Thanks, I think. Um, yes. I had a nightie picked out to put on last night, but we didn't make it that far. This morning I put on my flannel pajamas before getting ready for work because the house is cold in the morning and I thought that if I put on something sexy you might get distracted."

"What kind of panties are you wearing right now?"

Sean was driving and it was getting harder and harder to pay attention to the road. He wasn't sure that it was really smart to ask about her panties or what she was wearing that moment. He might have to pull over and get a hold of himself.

"I have on pink lace panties that match my pink lace

bra, and if you play your cards right, I will show them to you tonight," Maddy said very slowly.

"I'm a good card player." Sean replied.

And he was. He knew that the night was going to end with them in bed together again. It had been inevitable all day. At first, the flirting had been fun and playful, but the flier and name calling had changed the tone of the day. Now instead of going out, they would spend the night in, making dinner together, watching a movie, and cuddling on the couch. Their night would be much more intimate, which would lead to a, hopefully, much more passionate night spent in each other's arms.

Maddy wasn't nervous about her time with Sean, at all anymore. There was something about being with him after this afternoon that felt different. It was as if his seeing her with that flier had changed something between them—and it was better. She knew that she could trust him to treat her kindly about things and to make her laugh when she was upset and wanted to wallow a bit.

The panty conversation in the car had taken her mind off of the flier and made her feel desirable and wanted in a special way that only Sean had been able to do. She loved that he had found her sexy in her flannel pajamas that morning. It was nice to think that a guy could find her sexy in her regular stuff, not just her sexy stuff. They pulled up to the house and she waited for Sean to open her door. He was a gentleman and always opened every door for her. As she stood, he pulled her to him and kissed her.

"I'm sorry for being so inquisitive about your panties, and such. That really wasn't very well done. I think the thought of you in some sexy thing short circuited something in my brain. I just couldn't get passed it, until I talked about it. I'm better now, I promise." He kissed her again and then held her hand as they walked into the house.

"You're better now?" Maddy said as they walked into the family room. "Does that mean you don't want to see my panties, anymore?" After the emotions of the afternoon, she just wanted to be with him. She wanted to know that he was hers and that he wanted her. That he didn't believe that flier and didn't think that she was a tease. She would show him that she would definitely follow through. Slowly, she took off her coat and sweater as she walked farther into the living room. She turned to make sure that Sean was following her—he was. After throwing her coat and sweater across a chair, she stood in the middle of the room and slowly lowered the zipper on her dress. "Sean, you didn't answer my question."

Sean walked up to her and lowered the dress from her shoulders. He pressed small kisses along the same path the fabric took and along her collarbone. "That's not what that means, at all. I'm dying to see your panties."

With that, he pulled the dress the rest of the way off

of her body and she stepped out so that she was standing in front of him in her pink panties, bra, and silver high heels. Sean let out a groan. "Damn, woman. They say that a redhead shouldn't wear pink, but whoever the hell they are is very wrong. You are the sexiest thing I've ever seen."

Maddy knew that he had probably seen sexier, but she also knew that she had never felt sexier in her whole life. Sean put his hands on her hips and pulled her in close. She could feel his erection through his jeans and she leaned into it a little harder. They both moaned. Maddy pulled Sean's head down to hers and kissed him like she never would be able to again. She couldn't get enough of his mouth. Suddenly, he lifted her and she wrapped her legs around his waist. His hands found their way to her ass and he walked until he had her back up against the living room wall. "I'm not going to be able to last long. Do you want to do this here or upstairs?" he asked roughly.

"Here," was all Maddy could say. She barely could get the word out between kisses. She never wanted to stop kissing him, except she really wanted him undressed and she didn't think they could manage that with her wrapped around him. Slowly she lowered herself from him, sliding all of her against all of him. "We need to get these clothes off of you."

Sean practically ripped his sweatshirt and T-shirt off.

The jeans and tennis shoes took a little longer, but soon he stood in front of her in black boxer-briefs and Maddy thought she might pass out from the sexy sight in front of her. His body was magnificent. He spent his days playing around on the Internet, but obviously he took care of himself, too. There wasn't an inch of fat on his abs and she traced the ridges with her fingers.

Maddy put her hands on the sides of his boxer-briefs and quickly pulled them off, leaving Sean completely naked.

"Now you need to catch up," he said, while unhooking her bra and removing her panties. "Leave the heels on—those are sexy."

Now they were both naked in her living room and Maddy had to pause for a moment just to think for a second. She had Sean Walker, naked and hard, in her living room.

Sean broke her thoughts by kissing her. "Come back, Maddy. I could see the thoughts crossing your face. If you want to slow down, just tell me."

Maddy smiled and kissed him back. "I don't want to slow down. I was just thinking about how I finally have you naked, all mine, and how amazing this is going to be."

Sean laughed and ran his hands up her body. Slowly he caressed her breasts and ran his fingers across a puckered-up nipple, then he took her other nipple into his mouth. Maddy grabbed his hair and held his head to her chest. She could feel her bones melting from the sensations he was causing with his mouth. His hands were everywhere and she wasn't sure if she was going to be able to do anything other than stand there and let him pleasure her.

The sensations he had caused had her three quarters of the way to an epic orgasm and she wasn't in a place to really be judging anyone for their lack of foreplay, since she had done nothing for him. Sean leaned over and grabbed a condom out of his wallet. He quickly put the condom on and entered her.

Maddy gasped at the feeling of being filled by Sean. There was something different and right about being with him. It was like they were the perfect fit for each other. She didn't feel like he was too big or too small. Great, now she was thinking like Goldilocks, but about penis size instead of bed size. Then Sean started moving and she didn't think at all.

ↁↁↁ

Sean had never been with someone who felt so right. They had made love, and Sean knew that's what it had been, three times during the night. In between, they had made grilled cheese sandwiches and tomato soup and watched *The Hangover*.

As far as first dates went, it had been the best first one ever. Sean looked across the bed, saw Maddy's hair on the pillow, and smiled. She wasn't a peaceful sleeper. From the moment she fell asleep, she was wiggling and moving around. The only time she was still was when he was holding her, which wasn't a hardship for him at all. Sean thought about waking her up, but he knew this was the only morning when she got to sleep in so he was just going to enjoy watching her sleep for a little bit longer and then get up and make her breakfast in bed again.

Sean woke up again three hours later, shocked that he had fallen asleep. The week of moving, and nights of making love, had worn him out more than he had thought. He looked over and Maddy was no longer in bed with him. He got up, pulled on his boxer briefs, and set off to find Maddy.

She wasn't hard to find. She was in the kitchen, cooking breakfast and singing along with the radio. Sean stood in the doorway for a few minutes just watching her. She had pulled on his sweatshirt and nothing else. She looked sexy as hell.

There was a war going on in him between wanting to grab her and carry her back upstairs or to eat the delicious breakfast she was making. His stomach rumbled loud enough to catch her attention and it settled his internal debate.

He walked into the kitchen and caught her around the

waist. Sean might be starving for food, but he was also starving for a kiss from Maddy. He couldn't seem to get enough of her. After kissing her until they were both breathless, he stepped away. "Good morning, Mads."

"Good morning, Sean." She smiled up at him and he felt it all the way to his toes. He still didn't understand why he hadn't seen her this way for so long. It didn't make sense to him that she had been right in front of him and he had missed it. He was a smart guy.

"I made bacon and pancakes for breakfast."

"That sounds delicious," he replied, but she had turned around and he was focused on how the sweatshirt was riding high on her thighs.

They sat at the small table in her kitchen, shared breakfast, and talked about what they would be doing that day. Hank was coming over to help Sean move in his big stuff and the movers were supposed to be there with his bed and his office stuff later that day. One room on the third floor would be his office space and the other would be his bedroom.

Although he was hoping that he'd spend most of his nights with Maddy, and he could tell from the look in her eyes that she felt the same. Maddy was planning to help him most of the day, but then she had plans with the girls that night.

They were going to the Blood Moon for her employee's twenty-first birthday and then Cassidy, Fiona, and

Maddy had planned on staying afterward to play pool and hang out. Sean had hoped that he and Maddy would be spending another night cuddled up together or in bed together, but after how upset she had been the night before, he was glad that she wanted to go out with friends and not hide at home. They finished their breakfast and he pulled her upstairs to enjoy a little more alone time before Hank showed up to help him move in.

Chapter 15

S o Sean was being pretty sweet and protective of you yesterday," Cassidy said as they sat at a little corner table in the back of the Blood Moon. They had celebrated Annie's twenty-first birthday with her, and now Fiona, Cassidy, and Maddy were hanging out, waiting for a pool table to open up.

"He was. I overreacted to the flier, but he made sure I knew that none of it was true and then took care of me when we got home. We made soup and grilled cheese sandwiches, watched a movie, and cuddled." And had some pretty wild monkey sex around the house, Maddy thought to herself.

"Dinner, movie, and cuddling? Is that all you did?"

Fiona asked with a distinct tone of disapproval. "I'm pretty sure that you aren't blushing because of cuddling."

"Okay, and we did it. We had wild monkey sex, like you told me to, around the house. It was fantastic and I would much rather be doing that again right now than hanging out with you two talking about it. Are you happy?"

Fiona smiled. "Yes, I am."

Cassidy laughed. "Well, I don't like the idea of thinking about my brother having sex, yuck, but I'm happy for the two of you. I loved the way he was trying to make you laugh yesterday as if it was the most important job he had ever had in his whole life. He really was amazing and it was a side of Sean I hadn't seen before."

Maddy sighed. He had been amazing at the coffee shop and even better when they got home.

"Well, anyway," Fiona said. "We are both glad that you finally got the right man to wise up. I'm sure that it would have happened eventually, but I think I speak for all three of us when I say that I'm glad it happened now and we didn't have to wait any longer."

They clinked their margarita glasses and took a drink. A pool table opened up and they jumped on it before someone else could. It was Maddy's turn to get drinks, so she made her way to the bar and sat on the only available stool. They had already had more than they should, since they had started with champagne at Annie's party, but if they couldn't drive, one of them usually called Hank, or there was someone to give them a ride This was why girl's nights always took place at their house, so they didn't have to think about the logistics of getting home. Maddy was still waiting for Mike, the bartender, to notice her when someone came up and stood right against her back.

At first she thought it might be Sean, but she knew in an instant that it wasn't him. She would know the feel of his body against hers. and this wasn't it. Whoever the person was, he had a problem with respecting personal space. She was just about to turn around and let the jack hole know just what she thought of him rubbing his body against hers, when he leaned over and whispered in to her ear.

"Did you miss me, Maddy, darling?"

Maddy quickly jumped up, spilling the beer of the person sitting on her left. "Reid, what are you doing here?" she asked the man who had seconds before been rubbing himself against her right side and was now looking at her with lust and something dangerous in his eyes.

"I saw you were out with the girls and thought I would surprise you." He was dressed up in a suit and looked like the respectable veterinarian that she had thought he was, instead of a creepy stalker.

Maddy looked for Fiona and Cassidy, but they couldn't see her from the pool tables. They wouldn't be able to see that she was upset and she needed help. She didn't know what to do. There was obviously something wrong with Reid Mitchell.

He was the one who had called her a whore and a cock-tease on those fliers, which he had to have known she had seen, and now he was acting like there was nothing bad between them and that they were some sort of couple? And why the hell hadn't that spell worn off or broken or whatever it was supposed to do? Now would be the perfect time to know how to turn someone into a toad.

She was going to learn how to do that before she went out again. "Well, you did surprise me but, Reid, I'm hanging out with the girl's tonight. No boys allowed. You understand, right?"

"Of course, darling. I'll just sit here and wait for you to finish with the girls and then we can go back to my place." His smile looked sweet, but Maddy could see something darker just beneath it.

"Um, okay," she said while sprinting away.

"What's wrong?"

"Where are our drinks?" They said at the same time.

Maddy sat on a stool. She could feel her hands shaking. "Cassidy, I need you to call Sean and ask him and Hank to come down here. Don't tell them anything is wrong. Just ask if they want to play pool with us like we did the other night. They are at my house working on Sean's rooms."

Was that her voice that sounded so small and insignificant?

Cassidy pulled out her phone and did as Maddy asked.

"They are on their way. Sean admitted that they were about to crash our party, anyway. Now tell us what's going on."

"Reid is over at the bar. He leaned up against me and acted like we were a couple. Told me to have fun with the girls and then we could go back to his place. I played it off like that was fine and that we would after I hung out with you guys for a while, but I'm scared."

Both Fiona and Cassidy stood up and moved so they had a clearer look toward the bar. Reid waved to them and they sat back down. "He's still there. Do you think he realizes that we would call Sean or is he so delusional that he really believes that you are a couple?"

"I don't know. It seemed like he really believed that we were a couple and I don't know why after that flier he posted around town yesterday calling me a whore. Hopefully, once Sean and Hank get here he will leave. Until then let's just pretend he isn't there and play our game like we normally would. I didn't get our drinks, but we can wait till the guys get here and make them get them for us."

"Okay, we will follow your lead," Fiona said. "But I wouldn't count on him just leaving when Sean shows up.

He seems unstable. Maybe we should call the police?"

"No," Maddy said. "Let's just wait for Sean and Hank. Hopefully, Reid will go away. If we call the police, it will become a huge thing. I'm afraid that will make Reid even angrier and he will do something drastic. Let's just play and wait it out."

They played pool and waited for the guys to show up. Maddy tried to discretely keep tabs on Reid, but he didn't move from the bar stool he was sitting on and he made sure that she knew he was watching her. He sent drinks over for her, Fiona, and Cassidy and they accepted them, not wanting to anger him or upset him in any way.

While Cassidy was lining up a shot, Maddy pulled Fiona aside. "I think this is because of the damn spell. For some reason, it isn't breaking for Reid and he's still infatuated."

"I agree. I think it's probably because he wasn't stable to begin with. I think we need to step up the research and find a reversal spell. It will be harder to look at home now that Sean is there, but we can search the books at the store and I will talk to Great Aunt May. She may know of something, and if I tell her the whole story, she may be willing to help us out some. I think we need to get this figured out, and sooner rather than later."

Cassidy had finished her shot and rejoined them. "Is Reid still watching you?"

"Yes. I'm hoping that brother of yours gets here

soon." Just as Maddy said the words she felt a shift in the air behind her. She knew it was Sean and she felt better instantly.

He grabbed her from behind and placed a kiss on her neck. "What's going on?" he whispered in her ear.

She turned around in his arms to face him and to look to see where Reid was. He was still sitting at the bar, but where his earlier looks at her had been warm, even though they were creepy, now his face was cold and scary. Maddy shivered and Sean ran his hands up and down her arms.

"I will tell you, but you have to promise not to do anything stupid."

Hank had caught up with Sean and both men exchanged a look. "Maddy, if you have to preface something with that type of statement, then I will most likely do something stupid."

"Okay, but listen to me all the way before you do anything. At least promise me that."

"I promise," Sean said with a smile.

"Reid Mitchell is here." Sean started looking around, but Maddy grabbed his head and made him focus on her. "He came up to me at the bar and rubbed up against me. Then he acted as if we were a couple and I would be going home with him after I hung out with the girls tonight. It was very odd and made me uncomfortable. I could have dealt with it, but there was something in his eyes that was dangerous and made me feel unsafe."

Sean sat still for a second, but then he grabbed her hand and held it in his. "Did he see Hank and I come in?"

"Yes, and his demeanor changed. He looked downright evil after he saw you."

"Is he still here?"

Maddy couldn't see him from where she was standing, but she looked over at Fiona and Fiona shook her head. "He left when Maddy started talking to you. I'm sure he knew that you would be upset by what she had to say and he knew that he had to get away before you came to talk to him."

"Well, he was at least smart in that," Sean said. After looking at Maddy's worried face, he pulled her closer. "I'm not going to do anything stupid. In fact, I'm going to stay here with you, have a couple of beers, and play a game of pool. After that, we will go home."

Left unsaid was what they would do when they got home. Maddy hoped that they would be sharing a bed. She didn't care what they did, but she didn't want to sleep alone. "That sounds like a good plan, Sean."

Hank had left, probably to make sure that Reid had indeed left, and Cassidy had gone with him. Fiona went to get drinks.

Sean and Maddy were left on their own and Maddy decided that she wanted to have a little bit of fun on what was left of her Saturday night.

"Wanna play a game of pool, Sean?" she asked, trying to sound innocent.

"Okay," he answered.

"Let's play for stakes."

"What do you want to play for?"

"I was thinking a kiss for each ball you get in the pocket and the winner gets to pick their own prize."

"A kiss for getting your own balls in the pocket or just any ball?"

"Your own balls, Sean. You wouldn't win if you were only concerned with getting every ball in the pockets. I wouldn't mind getting lots of kisses, but I really want to win."

"What will you choose as your prize if you do win?"

"You mean when I win?" Maddy laughed. "I'm not sure, but it will have something to do with you and a bed, I'm sure."

"I think when I win, my prize will involve you and a bed too—or maybe the lounge chair in my office. I've had a fantasy for a long time about making love to someone in that chair, but it has never been woman specific. Today when I was moving it in and then rearranging it in my office, I couldn't help but think about you coming into my office and distracting me while I was attempting to work. The chair played a very prominent role in my thoughts."

"We better start playing the game."

"Are you getting too distracted?"

"Not me," Maddy said, but inside, she was a ball of desire. If Sean had asked her to leave right then, she would have been out the door with him. At that moment, she would have gone anywhere and done just about anything with him. All the talk about kisses and office furniture fantasies had completely taken the focus off of Reid, which had been her plan.

Sean let Maddy go first and she sank two balls into the pockets before missing a shot. Sean didn't waste any time giving her two unbelievable kisses. They were just ending the second kiss when Fiona, Cassidy, and Hank came back to their table.

Hank immediately started teasing them. "Can't you two play pool without making out?"

Maddy felt herself start to blush, but Sean just pulled her close and said, "With Maddy, I think it would always be the right time to make out. But if you must know, we are playing for stakes. Each ball in the pocket gets a kiss and the winner gets to pick their prize."

"Why can't I ever find a game like that?" Hank lamented to himself.

Everyone laughed. Hank was a great-looking guy who did all right with the ladies. Maddy thought it was because there was one in particular that Hank wanted and didn't realize it yet.

"So, who's winning?" Cassidy asked.

"We just started, but I've already got two balls in. I'm just not sure that Sean can catch up," Maddy joked.

Sean smiled as he took a spot beside the pool table and lined up his shot. "I don't think it really matters who gets the most balls in, we will both be winning this game."

Sean then proceeded to hit six of his seven stripped balls into the pockets in one turn. "You owe me six kisses, but I'm sure that everyone would appreciate it if I collected later."

"I know I would." Cassidy said. "I might be okay with my brother and best friend dating, but I don't want to watch them make out—ever."

Maddy really wanted to win, so she had to get her other five balls in this time. She tuned everyone else out and really concentrated. Lining up the shot, she hit the cue ball and watched as the ball moved slightly on its own to get just where it needed to be to connect and glide right into the pocket. Maddy had been whispering for the ball to move and it had. She tried it again with the next ball and the same thing happened. Maddy was able to get all five balls, plus the eight ball, into the pockets and win the game on that one turn. Everyone was cheering for her, but Maddy knew that something was going on.

Sean came over to her and gave her a big kiss. "I'll give the rest to you later. That was pretty impressive."

Maddy thanked him and then excused herself to go

to the restroom. She was a little shaken up from being able to move the ball by wishing for it. More and more, she was able to do things with her witchcraft that she had never thought she would be able to do. It was strange and made her uncomfortable.

As she walked down the hallway that lead to the restroom, Maddy was overcome with a feeling of unease. She raised her eyes and came face to face with Reid.

"Reid, what are you doing here. I thought you had left."

"I know you did. I saw Hank and Cassidy look for me. I hid out until they went back to the pool table where you and that asshole were busy making me look like a fool. What are you doing, Maddy? The whole town thinks you are a whore. Going from guy to guy. I'm the only one who is going to accept you and even I won't wait around forever. Sean is just using you for a convenient lay and, when he finds someone better, he will move on."

Maddy looked around, but didn't see anyone who would come to her rescue. She stood straight and looked him right in the eyes.

She didn't need to be rescued. She wasn't going to let this man, who had to corner her, call her names, and be mean to her because he didn't get what he wanted, upset her anymore.

"Reid, I don't know why you are so fixated on what

I'm doing, but it needs to stop. I'm with Sean and will be for the foreseeable future. You and I were never a couple. We never even went on a date. That means that you get no say in what I do or who I see. I don't believe you that anyone in town thinks I'm a whore. I went on a few dates and that was it. Now I'm dating a guy that everyone knows I've had a thing for since high school."

"You are already living with him."

"No, he's renting the top floor apartment of the house that I share with my cousin." Not that it was any of his business, but she was hoping that if she was forthcoming and blunt, he would get the message and leave her alone. "Will he be sleeping in my bed? God, I hope so. Or maybe I'll be sleeping in his. But that isn't any of your business. In fact, nothing I do is your business. So please, leave me the hell alone."

Maddy tried to walk away, but Reid pushed her into the wall and pushed himself against her. "I will not leave you alone. We are meant to be together. You may not have realized it yet, but I know it and you will, too. I'll allow you to have this little thing with Sean, but I know it won't last long. You aren't the kind of girl to keep his interest for long. If you were, he would have started dating you a long time ago." Then Reid kissed her hard before walking away.

Maddy sank to the floor and began to cry. She blamed herself for the place she was in. She knew that part of the problem was her spell, but she didn't deserve to be treated the way Reid had just treated her. She had been assaulted and now she had to go out and try to act normal. She didn't want Sean to know what had happened, but as she saw him coming down the hall, she knew she wasn't going to be that lucky.

Sean stood in front of her and watched her for a moment. She tried to smile, but couldn't, and it made the tears fall faster.

He pulled her to her feet. "Maddy, what's wrong?"

"It was Reid."

A dark look, unlike any she had ever seen, crossed Sean's face. "Where is he?"

"He left. This time, for sure."

"What did he do? You're crying." Sean wrapped his arms around her and pulled her tight. "Please tell me, Maddy."

Maddy put her head on his shoulder and took a deep breath. "He was mad about you being here and us flirting at the pool table. He said I was making a fool out of him and that everyone in town thinks I'm a whore." Sean started to interrupt, but Maddy didn't let him. "I told him that I know that no one in town believes that I'm a whore. I also told him that he has to leave me alone. That there isn't any way this is his business who I'm dating, sleeping with, or anything. I even told him that, yes, you are living in my house—on the third floor, but that I hope you spend every night in my bed or that I'm in yours. That's when he got mad." She wanted to stop there, but didn't. It would be wrong to not tell Sean the whole story. "Reid pushed me into the wall and kissed me. It wasn't a kiss meant to be sweet or loving. It was an assault."

"Dammit," Sean swore. "Are you okay? Did he hurt you in any other way?"

"My back hurts where I hit the wall, but I'm sure it's nothing. I just want to go home. And I don't want anyone else to know what happened. Fiona and Cassidy will freak out and never leave me alone."

"Well, I don't think you should be alone while Reid is bothering you. And I really think you should let them know what's going on, but you don't have to do that right now. I'll call Hank and tell him we are leaving. He'll think that we can't wait to be alone and so will they."

Maddy smiled. "I can't wait to be alone."

"Me, either, but just so that I can make sure you are really okay. We are going to get you home and I'm going to run you a bath. Then you can just lay there and relax."

"Are you going to join me?" she asked.

"Would you want me to? I thought you might just want to be alone."

Maddy shook her head. "I want to be with you."

Sean called Hank, told him they were leaving, and grabbed Maddy's hand. "Do you need to get anything or are you ready to go."

"I'm ready."

They left the Blood Moon and headed back to Maddy's. She wanted to be alone with him and forget everything that had happened with Reid.

Sean took Maddy home and helped her inside the house. He was struggling to keep his calm, but knew that the last thing Maddy needed was for him to lose it over the whole Reid situation. From the moment he had gotten to the Blood Moon and she had told him about Reid bothering her, Sean had been upset, but knowing that Reid had actually hurt her, made Sean want to punch somebody or something.

"Do you want a glass of wine with your bath?"

Maddy smiled at him. She still looked upset, but her color was returning and the smile was genuine, not forced. "No, I think I'll grab a bottle of water. I don't think I need anything else to drink tonight. I'm going to go put on my robe. Will you start the water?"

"I will. Is there anything special I need to do?"

"On the first shelf right by the tub there are some bath bombs. Put in the big yellow one. It smells like apples and cinnamon. It's my favorite."

Sean had no idea what a bath bomb or what it did, but if Maddy wanted one in her bath then she would get one. He followed her upstairs and into her bedroom before going into her en-suite bathroom. The bathroom had been updated recently and had a giant Jacuzzi tub in one corner. He could imagine Maddy sitting in there on many nights with a glass of wine and a romance novel. In the last few days, he had learned how much she enjoyed treating herself. When he looked on the shelf where she had said the bath bomb would be, there was a large basket full of them, along with several different bath salts, bubble baths, and bath oils. He also had found a drawer in her room that was full of chocolates and other treats. Maddy liked to indulge and Sean wanted to be the one to spoil her in any way he could.

When Maddy came into the room, wearing nothing but her green silk robe, he had her bath water ran with the bath bomb in it. The room was fragrant with the smell of cinnamon. Sean had also turned the lights down low and lit a few candles he had found around the room, which were also cinnamon. It was a romantic bath and Sean hoped that it set the mood and would take her mind off of everything she had to go through during the night.

Sean watched as Maddy slid off her robe and stepped into the tub. Maddy was the sexiest thing he had ever seen. He could see a bruise forming on her shoulder where Reid had pushed her into the wall and it took everything he had not to punch something.

"Is the water okay?" he asked, hoping that his voice didn't betray his feelings.

She smiled up at him. "It's perfect, but there is something that would make this bath better."

He sat on the floor beside the tub, picked up her sponge thing, and started running it up and down her arm. "And what would that be, sweetheart?"

"Well, I wouldn't mind if you took off your shirt."

Sean unbuttoned his plaid shirt and took it off. "Anything else?" Maddy was staring at him and it made everything in Sean tighten. He wanted to pull her from the tub and on top of him. To kiss every inch of her exposed skin, to sink into her, and banish all thought from both of their heads.

"I think you should take off everything else and join me in here."

She pulled up her legs as she asked him to join her. There was plenty of room in the oversized tub for the two of them. Sean had never been a bath guy. In fact, he couldn't remember the last time he had taken one, probably when he was five, but if there was a sexy woman like Maddy waiting for him in the tub, he would take one every night until the end of time. He stood and took off the rest of his clothes. Maddy was watching him, so he did everything much slower than he usually would. He loved that she seemed to like looking at him as much as he liked looking at her.

"Are you stripping for me, Sean Walker?"

"Yes, ma'am. Are you enjoying the show?"

She nodded and he could tell from her body's reaction that she was. Her breathing had sped up, a beautiful flush had spread across her breasts, and her glorious nipples were hard and begging to be loved.

"Is the water still warm? You aren't going to let me get in a cold bath, are you?"

"I promise you won't be cold," she said, and Sean knew that she wasn't talking about the water.

He got into the tub with her and pulled her into his arms. The bathtub was big, but not large enough for much movement on either of their parts with both of them in it. Sean extended his legs and Maddy lay on top of him. Their bodies lined up perfectly and Sean decided that this was one of the best ways to spend the night.

Maddy had never taken a bath with a man, but she was definitely seeing why they featured prominently in movies and romance novels. There was something sexy as hell about being with a man this way. She was lying across his body and could feel every part of him against her. It was somehow more intimate than laying with him in bed. Maddy raised her head to find his mouth with hers. She had a feeling that her encounters with Reid had affected Sean as much as they had her. Sean had always had a protective streak where she was concerned and, now that they were a couple, it seemed to have exploded. They both needed to be distracted and forget about what had happened at the Blood Moon.

"I want you," she said, as if he couldn't have figured it out by the way she had been rubbing herself on him.

"I want you too, Maddy." He pulled her face back
with his hands on both sides of her head. "Damn, you are
so beautiful. I just—I still can't believe I didn't see it before and I can't imagine not being with you. I'm so lucky
you finally told me how you felt and I pulled my head out
of my ass. I was so afraid of ending up like my parents,
or of ruining our friendship, that I couldn't see just how
perfect we are for each other. Maddy, I love you."

She wanted to tell Sean she loved him too, because
she did, but Maddy had that sick feeling in her stomach
again. This was all too perfect and too fast. Sean had
spent his whole life afraid of commitment. Afraid to be in
a relationship and now, after a week, he was confessing
his love? It had to be that fucking spell. Suddenly, Maddy
didn't feel so sexy and wanted. She felt stupid.

"Sean, I think I need to get out of the bath."

Maddy didn't wait for his reply or help getting out.
She very clumsily climbed out of the tub, grabbed her
robe, and ran out of the bathroom. Sean called after her,
but she ran to Fiona's room and shut the door.

How had she screwed her life up so much? How did
she get from "I want a man" to having the man of her
dreams telling her he loved her, but it not being real.
Maddy slid down on the other side of the door and felt
the tears start to run down her cheeks. She could still hear
Sean calling her name, but it didn't sound like he had left
her room yet. Maybe he would think she went down-

stairs. What was she going to do? There was no way for her to explain to Sean that she had cast a spell and that was why he loved her. He would think she had gone crazy. Suddenly Maddy knew what she was going to have to do. She was going to have to break up with him. It was the only way to break the spell. Maybe Sean would still like her a little and they could build on that relationship. Or maybe they would just go back to being friends and this small bit of a relationship would be all she ever had with him. Either way, it would be real and not driven by a spell. She couldn't do it tonight, though. Tonight, she needed to figure out a way to get him to go to his own bedroom and leave her alone.

Maddy was thinking so hard about what she was going to do that she was completely taken off guard when there was a knock at Fiona's door. "Maddy, sweetheart, are you in there?" Sean had found her and he sounded upset.

Maddy stood and opened the door. There were still tears in her eyes and she knew that she must look like the witch she was. "Sean, I'm sorry. I don't know what happened. I just freaked out."

He pulled her close. "Stop, Maddy. It's my fault. I shouldn't have told you I loved you after the night you had. I knew that you were in fragile place and I think it was just too much for you." He kissed her head and held her tight. "But I meant what I said. You don't have to say anything back or worry about what it means. I just want you to know that I meant it."

Maddy nodded her head, but didn't say anything. She couldn't. She wanted to say that she loved him too, that she had for a long time and that she really wished that he meant what he was saying. Instead she said, "I think I need to go to bed—alone."

Sean looked like he wanted to argue, but he didn't. He gave her another sweet kiss on the forehead and then left her standing in the hallway.

Maddy returned to her room and then the bathroom. She blew out the candles, let out the bathwater, and cleaned up the mess they had made. It was amazing how such a romantic moment could turn go from perfect to terrible so fast. Maddy needed to talk to Fiona, but she knew that the only way she was going to feel right was to break up with Sean so that she knew for sure his feelings were real. Of course, it wouldn't matter if they were, because she was going to lose him either way. If it was the spell that had him falling in love with her, he would simply move on when they broke up. If his feelings for her were genuine, she would be breaking his heart.

Chapter 16

The next morning Maddy found Fiona up earlier than normal and at the breakfast table waiting for her with coffee. Not only was it odd for Fiona to be up before Maddy, it almost never happened that Fiona made coffee for Maddy. She claimed that Maddy was too picky about how her coffee was made.

"Why are you up so early?" she asked while adding creamer to the coffee and sitting down at the table. Maddy knew that today would be a multiple cup of coffee day. She had gotten very little sleep the night before.

"I talked to Sean last night," Fiona said.

"You did?"

"Yes, he told me about what happened with Reid. He

said you asked him not to, but he thought I deserved to know since I live here."

"Sorry, I just didn't want you getting upset. He isn't going to do anything to you. It's me he's upset with and only me he will mess with."

Fiona sighed. "Don't you think that I would be upset if something were to happen to you—moron?"

"Of course." Maddy sighed. "That's not what I meant. I just didn't get much sleep last night and I'm not up to arguing this morning."

"I know. Sean a told me that you guys had, not quite a fight, but that something happened. Do you wanna talk about it?"

Maddy glanced toward the stairs. She did, but she was afraid that Sean would come downstairs and hear her. She didn't want him to hear her talking about him with Fiona, especially if they were talking about the Make Me a Match spell. "I do, but not here."

"If you are worried about Sean, he's not here. He went to Cassidy's about an hour ago. I think he needed to talk to someone and I'm too close to you to be a neutral party—of course, Cassidy might be, too."

Maddy was relieved that she wouldn't have to run in-to Sean before leaving for work. It made what she knew she had to do that night easier. "I have to break up with him."

Fiona slowly lowered her coffee cup and Maddy

could tell that she was shocked. "What do you mean? You *have* to break up with him? Did something happen last night between the two of you that was that bad?"

Maddy laughed. "No, in fact, if it weren't for that damn spell, what happened last night could have been one of the most perfect nights of my life. Sean brought me home, ran a bath with candles and everything, and then told me he loves me."

"Okay, Maddy, I'm not seeing anything that requires breaking up with the guy you have compared all other men to for as long as I remember."

"I couldn't say it back, Fi. He isn't saying it because he means it. He's saying it because he has to. The spell is causing him to feel this way. He said himself a few days ago that he never would have imagined being with me in a romantic way and that he had never planned on being in a relationship. Now he's telling me he loves me? He has to be under the spell and the only way to break the spell is to break up with him."

"You realize that if he isn't under the spell, you run the risk of breaking both of your hearts?"

"I know, but I can't be in a relationship where I don't believe him. It isn't fair to him or me."

"But are you sure that breaking up with him is the only way to know for sure, or is there another way?"

"Have you found a reversal spell? I haven't been lucky in any of my searches."

"I haven't found anything either. I'm going over to Miss May's later today to talk to her to see if she knows anything. With this Reid business, I know that she will help up out."

"I hope she knows something. She promised me that everything would work out, but right now I can't see how."

Fiona got up from her chair and walked around to where Maddy was sitting. She wrapped her arms around Maddy's neck and it made Maddy feel a bit better. Fiona and Maddy had always tackled the world together and this wouldn't be any different. If anyone could help her through this, it was Fiona. "I think he really does love you. I still think it's real and not a spell. I've always known there was something special between the two of you and, when he finally wised up, he would fall hard and fast."

"I wish I could just trust that, but I can't." Maddy felt the tears, that she thought she had shed all of the night before, come back. She closed her eyes. "I love him, Fiona. So much." Fiona froze. Maddy opened her eyes and looked across the room. Sean stood there, watching her. "Sean, how long have you been back."

"Long enough to hear that you don't believe that you can trust that I love you and that you love me. Why can't you trust me?"

Fiona stood and quietly left the room, leaving Maddy

to face Sean. This was the moment she had been dreading since last night. There was no way to tell him the truth, and no way to explain what she meant by that, without telling the truth. Maddy didn't know what to do. So she lied. "Sean, I know that you've dated a lot. I just don't think that you can be faithful and truly love one person. You haven't done it yet, so why would it be different now?"

Sean sat down hard. Maddy could see the hurt on his face. She wanted to take it all back. To tell him that she loved him, and he loved her, and that they would be happy together forever.

"Why would it be different now? Well, I thought it would be different because it was you. But now I'm thinking that nothing is different. That you are just like every other woman. You hold a man's past against him and act like he couldn't possibly change. I haven't ever been a serial dater, but when I moved back to Hollow Moon you were dating several different men at once. I never once thought you would be unfaithful to me because you were dating a lot. Why would you think the same of me? Maybe this is really because you want to keep dating. You said that you were dating because you thought you and I could never be together—because you had a crush on me that you thought would never be reciprocated. Well, it was. And now that you've made your conquest, you can move on to some other guy. Is that it? I told you that I was worried that our friendship wouldn't survive our dating, and I was right. Not only am I going to lose the woman that I've fallen in love with, I going to lose my best friend. You think I would do that for some other woman? You don't really know me."

"Sean, I don't want to date other people. I do love you. I just can't be with you. I just can't do this. I'm sorry. I'm breaking up with you."

Sean stood, sending the chair he had been sitting in flying backward, "I can't believe this, Maddy. I'll be at Hank's." He stormed out of the house, slamming the front door.

Maddy put her head down on the kitchen table and began to sob. She hated herself for what she had just done. She hated herself for casting the damn spell. She wished that she could go back in time and change it all. She would stop herself from casting the spell and from beginning this whole thing.

"Are you okay?" Fiona had come back in the room.

Maddy looked up with a little laugh and then put her head back down on the table. "Do I look like I'm okay? I just stomped all over him. I love him and I hurt him."

"He was hurt, Maddy."

"I'm aware."

"No. He was hurt. You broke up with him and he cared that you were doing it. You hurt him. If he had been under a spell, he wouldn't have cared one way or another. He would have just shrugged it off and walked away. But he didn't do that. He argued and he told you what he thought. Sure, he wasn't nice, but like I said. He was hurt."

Maddy thought about what Fiona said. It should make her feel better that Sean cared, but that meant that she broke up with him for no reason and that wasn't something she could cope with. "So I did it for no reason. I lost him and it was for no reason at all."

"Maybe you didn't lose him. Maybe he will calm down and the two of you will find a way to get past this."

Maddy just shook her head. With all of the issues Sean had had before starting a relationship with her, there was no way that he would get over her picking a fight with him. "Can you work for me today?"

"Of course. Why don't you go back to bed?"

Maddy nodded and headed back upstairs. She hoped that Sean would stay away for a while and that their paths wouldn't cross when he did come home. She couldn't see that look on his face again. Fiona hadn't seen it. Maddy knew she hadn't just broken them up—she had crushed his very small belief in happily ever after.

Chapter 17

Sean drove on auto pilot to the Crescent. He couldn't believe that Maddy had broken up with him and he was still a little confused on what exactly had happened. She had been telling Fiona that she couldn't trust in his feelings, but that she loved him too. He had been so happy to hear that she loved him that he hadn't realized at first what else she had said.

He wasn't sure what he had done that she felt she couldn't trust him. Sure these feelings had come on fast in their relationship if you thought of it from when they started seeing each other romantically, but they had been friends since they were teenagers. He knew everything about her and there wasn't anyone else he would share his deepest thoughts with.

There had been a time in the past when he had been known to date a lot, but that had been years before. In fact, Sean hadn't dated much in the last few years and, when he had started really seeing Maddy, he had realized it was because of her. These were the things he should have told her when she said she couldn't trust him, but instead he had lost it. He had only felt the hurt and let it out.

Getting out of the car, he wished that Cassidy had still been at home, but Hank would hear about what had happened, sooner or later. Sean still worried that there was a part of his best friend that wanted to be with the woman he was in love with. And, even though she didn't trust him, Sean was still very much in love with Maddy Simpson.

Cassidy spotted him as he walked in. He must have looked as bad as he felt, because she instantly came out from behind the counter and led him to a table. "What happened?"

He had shown up at her apartment at four-thirty that morning to talk to her about confessing his love for Maddy and Maddy's odd reaction. They had formed a plan for him to talk to Maddy, but he hadn't even gotten a word in before she had laid the bombshell down on him.

"Maddy and I broke up." Even saying the worlds

made his chest hurt. If this was what being in love did to people, then he wanted no part of it ever again.

"What do you mean you broke up? You came to my apartment this morning talking about being in love with her and I know that she is in love with you."

"Well, she might be in love with me. I'm not really sure if she is or she isn't. But she doesn't trust my feelings for her and doesn't think that she would ever be able to. She thinks that I'm just playing with her until I move on with someone else and that eventually I will break up with her. I guess she was just beating me to the punch."

A ding from Cassidy's pocket had her pulling out her phone. "It's Fiona. She was making sure that you had come here and letting me know that something had gone down if you hadn't. I'll text her back that you are here. Should I ask how Maddy is?"

Sean hated himself for caring, but he nodded. Cassidy's fingers flew on the keyboard of her phone and they both stared at it, waiting for the ding that would let them know how Maddy was doing. Sean hoped that she was at least as upset as he was.

After what felt like an eternity the phone dinged and Cassidy read the text. "Maddy is sobbing in her room. She broke up with Sean for what she felt was a good reason, but it devastated her."

"What the hell could be the good reason for breaking up with me? I've never given her any reason to think I

want to be with someone else. Hell, we've only been seeing each other a week. I told her that I never imagined us
being together like that and that it was amazing. Those
are the things I told her. I told her I loved her." Sean's
voice had escalated with each sentence. He could tell that
Cassidy was listening to him, but she was also texting
with Fiona. "What are you saying?"

"That you are losing your shit and that we have to
find a way to get the two of you back together."

"I don't know if that's possible. She broke my trust. I
told her why I don't do relationships and she threw it in
my face."

"And you didn't say anything hurtful to her?"

Sean thought about what he had said about her dating
habits when he arrived to town. He had practically called
her a whore. "I might have said something in anger.
Damn, I really need to talk to her."

"Good thing you live in the same house, but you
might want to give it a day or two. If she is really upset,
Maddy needs time to regroup. It's just her way. I know
that you are a charge-in-and-fix-it guy, but you can't be
that way this time."

"Cassidy, I don't know that I want to fix it. I honestly can't say that I want to be in a relationship with Maddy. This fighting, breaking up, her crying, us both upset—bullshit is not what I want. This is too much like
Mom and Dad. The drama isn't what I want."

"You just want the happy stuff. I get it. But, Sean, life doesn't work that way. I'm not saying that most of the time the perfect relationship wouldn't be rainbows and unicorns. It totally would be. But there are going to be times when you disagree or when you argue. If you don't, then the relationship is just as dysfunctional as one where all they do is argue and fight. If you can't put up with that, then you should probably leave Maddy alone for good."

Sean thought about what Cassidy was saying. He didn't want the drama, but he knew that she was right. It couldn't be perfect all the time, because he wasn't perfect and neither was Maddy. However, he wasn't sure that he was made to be in a relationship. "Can I crash at your place tonight? I will go back to the house tomorrow, but tonight I think I should stay out."

"Of course, you can. I wouldn't turn you away even if you are being dumb. But I will probably be out tonight. Fiona said that we are going to have an ice cream and vodka binge at their house. It's what we do when one of us is upset. Is it going to upset you if I go over there and hang out with Maddy? I promise not to trash talk you— too much."

"I wouldn't expect you to turn down ice cream and vodka for me, plus I'm sure Maddy would appreciate you being there. I know that this puts you in a bad spot— caught between the best friend and brother."

"I just want both of you to be happy. And I happen to believe that you would be happiest with each other. Now, I have to go back to work before Hank has a stroke. Is there anything else you need?"

"A big black coffee."

Sean thought about what Cassidy had said. That he and Maddy would be happiest with each other. He didn't know if he believed that. It was hard to think that way when he was still so shocked by how things had turned out today. Cassidy just wanted them both to be happy and he understood that, but Sean was going to have to really think about what would make him truly happy.

Hank came over with his coffee and Sean sighed. He didn't want to rehash what had happened. He put a smile on his face and thanked Hank for the coffee.

"Everything okay, Sean?" Hank asked.

"Yeah, just a late night." Sean tried to make it sound like his late night had been for a much happier reason than the reality. He didn't want Hank digging in and asking questions.

"Okay. You know I'm here to talk if you need to."

I must not be able to hide my feelings as well as I think. "I'm fine, Hank. No worries."

Hank left, but not before patting Sean on the shoulder. This was another thing that Sean wasn't used to. People feeling sorry for him. It was usually him who offered support to those around him. Not the other way around. He didn't want anyone to feel sorry for him. He wanted everything to go back to how it had been just a few days ago. He and Maddy making love in her room and nothing else getting in the way.

Sean was drinking his coffee and deep in thought when the very last person he wanted to see that morning sat down at his table—Reid Mitchell.

Reid Mitchell sat across from him, a smug look on his face. "So the whore dumped you, too? I knew she would. She loves nothing more than to conquer a man, make him love her, and then throw him away. You can join my group if you want to. We are going to mee—"

Sean didn't even wait for Reid to finish his rant against Maddy. He grabbed the other man by the shirt with his left hand and punched him in the face with his right. Reid fell back on the floor. Sean pulled him back up then punched him again. Hank ran over, but backed off at Sean's look. Sean could take care of this himself.

"You will not—" He punched Reid in the stomach. "—call Maddy—" Another punch. "—a whore." Sean pushed Reid back down into the chair and sat back down opposite him. "Do you understand?"

Reid nodded as the blood rushed out of his nose. Sean had broken the man's nose and probably given him a black eye, but he would not allow this prick to call Maddy names ever again and this was the only way he could think of to get his point across. "I think it's best if you stay out of the Crescent and Full Moon Books from now on. I can't tell you to stay out of any other part of town, but I can and will kick your ass if I see you in these two places. Do you understand that?"

Reid stood and started walking out, but before he left he turned and said. "Eventually, she will be mine."

Sean started to get up and go after him, but Hank and Cassidy were instantly by his side and stopped him from going. "You can't chase him into the street. You will get arrested. He could still press charges against you now. The only thing that will work in your favor is that he walked away, everyone saw him leave, and he started harassing you first. Why on earth did you attack him like that, Sean?" Cassidy asked.

"He called Maddy a whore—again. And after what he did to her last night, I just couldn't do nothing."

This time Hank asked the question. "What did he do to Maddy last night?"

"He pushed her into a wall. She has a bruise on her shoulder. And then he kissed her against her will. It really upset her. He is fixated on her and goes back and forth between saying terrible things about her and acting like they're a couple. He has a screw loose, for sure."

"I saw the flier where he called her a whore and a cock-tease, but I thought that was just because he was upset that she broke off their date. I didn't think it had escalated any further."

"Well, it did. And I'm not sure that I didn't just make it worse instead of better, but I couldn't help it. He called her a whore to my face and I saw red. I'm worried about what he might do to her now that he knows I'm not there to protect her. He knew we had broken up and it just happened. How could he have known that unless he is spying on her, somehow?"

Cassidy wrapped her arms around him, and he loved that his little sister was close enough to give him a hug when he really needed one. "I wish I had known all of that. I would have kicked him in the balls when he was hunched over from one of your punches to his ribs." All three of them laughed. "Where did you learn to fight so well, big brother?"

"I box twice a week, or at least I did in Boston. It was one of the ways I made sure I didn't get fat sitting at a computer for twelve hours a day." He looked down at his knuckles. They were all scrapped up and bleeding. "I better go clean this up. Hank, if anything is damaged or broken, I will pay for it."

They looked around, but didn't see anything that looked broken.

"Everything is good, man. Even if you had broken something, I wouldn't care. It was in defense of our Maddy and that would be worth a broken chair or two."

Cassidy, who had left to get her keys, came back and handed them to Sean. "Here are my keys. You can hang out at my place for as long as you want. Don't let Maddy see your hands looking like that. I'm not sure how she would feel about you hitting someone, even Reid, in her defense."

Sean would hope that she would appreciate it, but today had proved that he didn't know jack about women.

Chapter 18

It had been ten hours and thirty five minutes since Maddy had broken up with Sean and she was still waiting for the shock to wear off. She wanted to feel like she was right for just a moment, and like she hadn't just ruined her whole life, because she was scared.

Luckily, Cassidy and Fiona were working hard to make sure that she wouldn't feel anything for the rest of the night.

They were giving her shots and Cassidy had brought several different types of ice cream. It was the ritual for when something bad had happened.

"Here's another shot." Cassidy handed it to her and took one for herself. "One, two, three."

They both shot the drink and Maddy felt the alcohol burn down her throat. This was shot number three and she was finally starting to feel a little numb, however, she still couldn't get the image of Sean's face out of her head. It was going to take a lot of alcohol to make her forget.

"So you wanna tell me what's really going on here or do you need more to drink first?" Cassidy asked.

"What do you mean? What did Sean tell you?" Maddy really wanted to know what Sean would have told his sister, but she hated putting Cassidy in the middle.

"He said that you broke up with him because you didn't trust his feelings. I think that's bullshit. I don't know why you couldn't trust his feelings or what that's about, but you've been in love with him forever, and I can't imagine you not fighting for him with everything you've got."

Cassidy was right that, under normal circumstances, Maddy would have fought for Sean. She would have fought for him to the bitter end, but this was different. She would have been fighting against her own fears and it would have been a losing battle. "I just couldn't get past his past."

Cassidy looked like she was going to argue, but Fiona stopped her with her with another shot. "No more talk about men. At least real ones. Let's talk about a fictional one who can't upset us."

Maddy was so grateful for her cousin. Fiona knew why Maddy couldn't tell Cassidy the truth and she was trying to help distract her away from talk of Sean.

They all did another shot and talk turned to the hero in one of their favorite book series—Roarke.

"He's dreamy," Cassidy said with a slight slur, while eating another spoonful of her strawberry ice cream.

Maddy took another shot and felt the room spin. "He wouldn't care if Eve was a witch and cast a spell that made all the men fall in love with her."

Cassidy and Fiona both looked over at her. "What?"

"Nothing."

Cassidy kept looking at her, but Maddy didn't say anything else.

"He would beat up a guy who wronged Eve, kind of like Sean," Cassidy said and then quickly covered her mouth.

"Who did Sean beat up?" Fiona asked.

"No one," Cassidy said, but she was looking at the ceiling and they had been friends long enough for Maddy to know that meant she was lying.

Maddy did another shot and handed one to Fiona and Cassidy. She waited for them both to take it and then she asked Cassidy, "Who did Sean beat up?"

"Ugh, you aren't going to leave me alone until I tell you, are you?"

"Nope. I'm not," Maddy said, laying her head down

in Cassidy's lap. She probably should have stopped two shots ago.

"Sean was in the Crescent today and Reid Mitchell said something about you that Sean didn't like. Then Sean kicked his ass."

Maddy sat up so quickly the room spun around and around before settling. "Sean beat up Reid? Like really beat him up?"

"Reid had a broken nose and I'm sure a black eye. Plus, I bet his ribs hurt like hell. Sean really let him have it. Then Sean made Reid sit down and promise that he would never call you names or come into the bookstore or coffee shop again. It was pretty epic."

Maddy thought about what Cassidy had just said. It was pretty amazing to have a guy beat up somebody else for you.

Fiona smiled. "I told you he likes you," she said in a sing-song voice.

"Of course, he does, dumb ass," Cassidy said. "He told you he loved you. Why did you think that he didn't like you?"

"Because of that stupid spell," Maddy said before she could stop herself and then everything stopped.

Fiona looked at her. Maddy shrugged. She was tired of hiding from Cassidy and maybe if she told her friend the truth, then Cassidy could help her figure out what to do.

Unless Cassidy thought she was crazy and that her brother had made a lucky escape.

"Um, spell, Maddy? That's the second time you've mentioned a spell. Have you been watching *Charmed* again?"

Cassidy had given her the perfect out and she could tell from the raising of Fiona's eyebrows that she wanted her to use the excuse, but instead Maddy told the truth. "I'm a witch and I cast a spell to find my perfect match."

Cassidy laughed, but when she noticed Maddy and Fiona weren't laughing too, she stopped. "What are you talking about? No more shots for you, Maddy." She laughed again. "A witch."

Maddy decided that she would have to do something to make her believe that she was a witch, but as drunk as she was, there wasn't a lot that Maddy was able to do. She could start a fire though. She looked over at the unlit fireplace in the corner of the family room and concentrated really hard. Suddenly a fire roared to life.

"Holy shit!" Cassidy yelled. "You are a witch."

Maddy nodded, but lighting the fire had worn her out.

Fiona spoke then. "We both are. It isn't something we talk about and we don't really even practice witchcraft. Maddy's first real spell was the Make Me a Match spell she cast two weeks ago that was supposed to bring her soul mate. But, when she was casting it, something went wrong and she ended up attracting all men."

"That's why everyone was asking you out and hitting on you all of a sudden. You are hot, but you have never attracted that kind of attention before."

"I know. Then Sean came back to town and the spell made him want me."

"No," both Fiona and Cassidy said at the same time.

"At least that's what I believed. The spell is broken by a refusal. If I turn down the date or in Sean's case, break up with him, then the spell is broken. I'm sure that's what happens. I broke up with Sean so that I could know for sure how he felt about me. I know that sounds wrong, but I couldn't live forever wondering if he was only with me because of the spell."

Cassidy smiled. "I get that. I wouldn't be able to either, but why couldn't you just tell him?"

Maddy laughed. "Tell him that I'm a witch and that I cast a spell and that might be why he loves me? Yeah, I'm sure he would believe me and that he would want to be with me after that."

"Okay, so maybe you couldn't say it just like that, but there has to be something you can do. I know that Sean really does love you and that you love him. There has to be a way to get the two of you back together."

Maddy shook her head. "No, I don't think there is, and it's okay. I messed up. You didn't see the look on his face. Sean was so sure before that a real relationship was a bad idea. Well, I just proved him right. He has been vindicated and that's pretty much what he said to me this morning. Plus, he also thinks that I want to date other people and that's the reason I broke up with him. He was pretty harsh—I totally deserved it—but I don't think he will forgive me any time soon."

"I wouldn't be too sure. I think he's going to come back sooner than you think." And with that prophetic statement Cassidy passed out.

Maddy curled up on the couch opposite of Cassidy and looked over at Fiona. "I'm sorry I blabbed."

"It's okay. She probably won't remember and, if she does, she will think it's cool. Plus, she has some witch's blood in her, so she could probably help us out if she wanted to. In fact, if she is cool with everything, I might ask her to look through some of her family's stuff and see if she can find anything that might help us."

Maddy smiled. She thought about Cassidy embracing her family's past and their witchy ways. She would be hell on wheels if she started casting spells. Of course, she couldn't be any worse than Maddy. No one could be worse than her, she thought.

"Do you really think I'll be able to work things out with Sean?" she asked Fiona.

"I hope so and I do think so, but it will take some time. I don't think it will happen as quickly or as easily as Cassidy seems to think."

Maddy didn't think anything about love was supposed to be quick or easy, but she wished that it would at least be a little bit more kind.

Chapter 19

A week and a half later, Maddy was still walking through the fog of loss. She hadn't seen Sean since he had left her house that morning, although she had heard him a time or two walking above her or leaving before she got up.

According to her sources, Cassidy and Hank, he spent most of his time at the library or Cassidy's apartment, and he was just as miserable as she was. While, in theory, that made her feel better, she hated the idea that he would be okay with them being apart.

She also hated that he was so hurt and upset by their breakup.

It meant that she was wrong and she had screwed up

what was probably the best thing to ever happen to her for absolutely no reason.

Maddy walked into the Crescent for the first time since the incident and was shocked to see Sean sitting at a table in the corner.

Cassidy had told her that he had been avoiding the coffee shop too, so Maddy had assumed that it would be safe to stop in quickly and pick up an extra huge triple shot espresso before she opened the book store that morning.

She hadn't slept at all the night before and she had to have something that would help keep her awake.

Cassidy called her over. "Maddy, I have what you texted me you needed."

Maddy hadn't texted anything, but she was willing to let Cassidy provide a distraction for her. Maddy had been frozen and didn't know if she should try and talk to Sean or not. At the counter, Maddy said, "Thanks, I needed some direction out there. I thought you said he wasn't coming in to the coffee shop anymore."

"He wasn't. This is the first morning he's come in since he had the fight with Reid."

"And since we broke up."

Cassidy nodded. "I honestly didn't think he would come back. Of course, I didn't think that you would come in either. What are you doing here?"

"I didn't sleep last night. I need a bucket of espresso with extra shots."

"I was looking through some of my family's books and I found a spell that is supposed to help with insomnia. We could try it—"

"No!" Maddy said a little too loudly, causing the whole coffee shop, including Sean, to look over at her and Cassidy. "We don't know enough about that stuff to cast a spell. With my luck, we would cast a spell to combat insomnia and I would end up sleeping for a hundred years."

Cassidy laughed. "That's true."

"So you're okay with all this witchcraft stuff?"

"I think it's awesome. The only thing I'm not okay with is that you didn't tell me right away. I would have loved to have been there when you cast the spell. It might have all gone differently if I had been there as backup."

"True."

"I asked my mom about our family's legacy and she said that my grandmother was a practicing witch, but that for some reason the gift didn't pass down to my mom. I think it might be the real reason she's so unhappy. She just can't tell anyone because it would make her sound crazy. So she takes everything out on my dad."

"Have you tried to do anything? To see if you are able to cast a spell or do anything witchy?" Maddy took a quick look around to see if anyone was listening to them, but the only person whose eye she caught was Sean's and he quickly looked away.

"I was able to light a candle with a spell and I can move things just by thinking about it. It's pretty cool. You, Fiona, and I could be our own little coven."

Maddy rolled her eyes. This was not how she pictured Cassidy taking this news if she ever heard about Maddy casting a spell and that Cassidy, herself, was a descendant of witches. But Maddy really should have known that Cassidy would think it was awesome.

"Are you going to tell your brother?"

"I don't know if I should or if you should."

"Me?"

"Well, it's the real reason you broke up with him, right?"

"Yes."

Cassidy's eyes got really big and Maddy knew that Sean had come up behind her. "What was the real reason you broke up with me, Maddy?"

"Shit," Maddy said. "I can't do this." And she ran out of the Crescent without her coffee and without her pride.

"What was the real reason she broke up with me, Cassidy?" Sean asked, watching through the windows of Crescent Coffee as Maddy sprinted down the sidewalk toward Full Moon Books.

"That's between the two of you and I'm not getting in the middle of it."

Sean knew that he shouldn't press his sister, but he wanted an answer and he wanted it now. It had been over a week since he had been able to even be in the same room as the woman he loved and it was driving him insane. He wanted nothing more than to figure out what had gone wrong and to fix it so she would be with him again. He wasn't mad anymore, wasn't even all that hurt. He just missed her and wanted her back.

"Please, Cassidy, just tell me. I can't fix this if I don't know what's really wrong. You don't have to tell me everything, just tell me the big thing that I can try to work with."

"What happened to not being sure about being in a relationship with her and not knowing if you were made to be with someone? Has that changed? You were pretty sure before that you couldn't be serious about being in a relationship. Now you want to know what is wrong so you can fix it? I can tell you one thing. That is that you don't talk to other people about your relationship. You need to talk to Maddy. If you have to chase her down or confront her at the house, then that's what you do. Working in your favor is the fact that you technically live together. It isn't stalking her, if you happen to be waiting for her to come home, when you live in the same house."

Sean laughed. "I guess you're right. I just want to be

with her again, Cassidy. I know that she's the one who broke up with me and I honestly don't think I did anything wrong, but I will do anything to get back with her."

"Good, because the two of you have been very hard to live with the last few weeks, and I liked it better when you were kissing than now when you're moping."

"I liked it better when I was kissing her, too," Sean said and then walked away.

Cassidy was right. He had been avoiding Maddy at the house, but he didn't have to do that. There was nothing that said he couldn't run in to her and, if he ran in to her several times over several days, maybe she would tell him what was going on and why she had really broken up with him.

There was a reason other than the one she had given him, that much was obvious. Sean didn't believe that she wanted to date other men or that she was worried he would want to date other women. It was definitely something else, and it was time for her to tell him so that they could work through whatever the problem was together.

Chapter 20

Maddy couldn't believe she had run away from Sean. She was behaving like a crazy person and it was starting to be ridiculous. She could have come up with a plausible reason there on the spot. She wasn't an idiot. He would have believed her and, even if he hadn't, he wouldn't have called her out on it. But, no, she had run out of the Crescent like the hounds of hell were chasing her and made an absolute fool of herself. Plus, she still didn't get the coffee she desperately needed.

It was Tuesday morning and Maddy had no idea if the romance books for Miss May and Miss Aggie had been pulled or if the new releases were ready to be placed on the shelves. These were things she could control. She would get a coke out of the refrigerator for her sugar and caffeine fix and hope like hell that it was enough to tide her over until Cassidy took her break and brought over her morning coffee. At least she had that to look forward to.

Maddy threw herself into the work and didn't look up until the bell above the door dinged over an hour later. Looking at her watch, Maddy sighed happily. It was Cassidy's break time, so the wonderful bell was probably Cassidy with delicious life affirming coffee. Maddy got off of her position on the floor, where she had been sorting books by year and author, and rounded the corner, but stopped suddenly when it wasn't Cassidy with coffee who had walked through the door, but the delivery man from Eclipse Flowers with a gorgeous bouquet.

"These are for you, Maddy," Frank said.

He had been delivering flowers for the shop he owned with his wife for over thirty years and this was the first time he had ever delivered flowers to Maddy.

Maddy took the flowers from him. It was a gorgeous bouquet of roses, lilies, and a flower she didn't recognize. "What kind of flower is that, Frank?"

"It's an iris."

Maddy looked at the flower. It was unusual and lovely. Frank left the bouquet and Maddy pulled the card out of the stems. She hoped that they were from Sean. This could be the initial step in their reconciliation. She opened the card and was shocked by what she read.

> *You don't have Walker to protect you anymore. He hates you as much as I do. I will make you pay for the way you used me and then threw me away.*

Maddy closed the note and held it in her trembling hands. It was from Reid—it had to be. He was the only one so angry at her and the only one who wanted to get back at her for something. This was the first outright threat and Maddy didn't know what to do about it. Should she take it to the police or just ignore it?

She wanted to call Sean and tell him about it, so that he could help her make the decision, but she'd given up that right when she had broken his heart. So, instead, she decided, for the first time, to close the bookstore and go home.

She would figure out what to do from there and maybe hide her head under the covers for a while, too.

Maddy knew that she was being a coward, but there was no way she was going to stay at the bookstore by herself for the rest of the morning and wait for Reid to pop up somewhere. She would be safe at home, with the door locked, under the covers of her bed. Plus, maybe Sean was home, since he would think she was at work for the day and he would be there to protect her. Sure, it was completely anti-feminist and weak, but she was scared. She wanted him to hold her and tell her that everything was going to be okay.

Maddy pulled in front of her house and looked around. Everything looked the same as it always did and she didn't see any indication that anything sinister had been happening at her home. She also didn't see Sean's car, so he hadn't come back from town yet. It was probably for the best, but Maddy was really ready to talk to him and settle some of the discord between them. She wanted to apologize and see if she could at least get some of their friendship back.

She got out of the car, walked into the house, and put her stuff down on the counter in the kitchen. She started to pull her cell phone out of her purse to call Fiona and find out where she was when she felt someone behind her.

At first, she believed that it was Sean, but that thought quickly vanished when the person grabbed her and threw her into the kitchen table with great force.

"You bitch. I knew that you would come running back here, hoping that he would take care of you, right?"

Maddy turned around to face her attacker, knowing who she would see there. Reid Mitchell was standing in her kitchen, looking as if he could kill her.

"I didn't come running to him. I came to my home because I was scared. Scared of you. You need help, Reid."

Maddy tried to inch her way toward the land line that Fiona had insisted they keep, even though neither of them ever used it. If Maddy could get to the phone and dial 911, someone would be there soon to save her. She just had to keep Reid talking and not paying any attention to what she was doing.

"I don't need any help. You do. You need to stop being such a whore and stop spreading your legs for every man in town." He lunged toward her and pulled on the arm of her T-shirt ripping the sleeve at the seam.

Maddy screamed and kicked at him. "I do not do that."

"You were dating me, sleeping with Sean Walker and who knows who else. I told him what you were really like. He didn't believe me and punched me in the face. But I've seen that you still aren't back together. I think he really knows what you are like and just didn't like me pointing it out to him. I wouldn't like anyone pointing out that my ex-girlfriend is a whore either."

Reid then grabbed Maddy and carried her into the front room. She made herself go limp so that she was heavier and harder to carry, but he was stronger than she'd thought he would be and could carry her with no problem. Maddy was really starting to panic. She didn't know what he was planning to do to her, but she didn't imagine that it was anything pleasant.

She decided to try and reason with him or maybe she should flirt with him. Maybe if she turned him on, he would be distracted and wouldn't want to hurt her. She could make him think that she wanted him.

At least she thought she could, maybe, make him think that. As long as her revulsion didn't show through her eyes.

"Reid, maybe I got everything wrong. Maybe I should have gone out with you. I know that going out with Sean was a mistake, but I think canceling our date was an even bigger one. I should have gone out with you. Given it a chance to see how things could have been between us."

Reid looked like he was listening to her and Maddy thought that maybe she had gotten through to him. Maybe she could get him calm enough to leave her alone. She was about to promise him a date when he turned on her again.

"Do you think I'm stupid?" He pulled her into him and grasped her jaw in his hands, hard enough that Maddy would have a bruise from his fingers the following day. "I know you are just trying to placate me. You don't want me. You just want to get away so that you can get help. I know that you find me repulsive. I can see it in your eyes, Maddy. Now, what am I going to do with you?" he asked as he kissed her and then ran his hands down her body.

Maddy was worried that he was going to sexually assault her and the only thing she could think of was to freeze him like she had Sean and Hank that day in the hallway. If only she had done that on purpose and knew how she had done it. It was something that had just happened and she had no idea how she had done it or if she could even do it again.

Reid ran his hand down her chest and roughly grabbed her breast. It hurt, and Maddy knew that if she didn't do something right that minute, it was going to be much worse for her very soon. She closed her eyes and focused all of her thoughts and energy on to freezing Reid. It didn't work.

Maddy began to fight in earnest. "Get off of me now!" she screamed, pushing at the same time. A surge of energy flowed through her. Reid went flying off of her and across the room, hitting the wall with a loud thud.

"How the hell did you do that?" he yelled at her.

"I'm a witch, jackass," she yelled back as she raised her hands and, feeling all the power that she had awakened when she threw him off of her, froze his ass.

That's when she looked up and saw Sean walking through the doorway.

చుచుచు

Sean had come back to the house and seen Maddy's car in the driveway. He hadn't known if he should go in or leave and go somewhere else until she left. But he was worried about her, because she should have been at work and not home at ten in the morning. Especially on Tuesday, which was one of her favorite days of the week, since that was when the new books came out and Miss May came into the store.

He had gotten out of his car and headed toward the house, when he heard shouting from within. Maddy wasn't alone and from the sound of her screams, whoever was with her wasn't there because she wanted them to be. Sean charged into the house but then froze at what he saw and heard.

Maddy was screaming, "I'm a witch, jackass."

Then she held up her hands and froze her attacker, who turned out to be Reid. She glanced up and locked eyes with Sean. She looked magnificent. Her eyes were blazing and she was shaking, but he couldn't tell if it was with fear or something else.

"What the hell did you just do?" he asked as he slowly walked into the room.

Maddy looked at him, but he didn't think she was really seeing him and he realized that she was in shock. "Maddy, sweetheart, what did you just do to Reid?"

She walked straight to Sean and wrapped her arms around his waist. "I froze him before he could rape me."

"Froze him?" Sean decided to focus on that instead of the fact that she was positive that Reid would have raped her.

"Shit," Maddy said with a sigh. "I guess there's no way to tell you that you aren't seeing that Reid is frozen, is there?"

"No, I'm definitely seeing a frozen dude. Can I punch him and he'll stay that way?"

Maddy laughed a small laugh and it made him feel like a god. He was making her feel a little bit better when things were obviously so awful.

"I think you probably could punch him," she said. "I was thinking about kicking him in the balls, but it seems kind of mean, since he can't defend himself."

"Screw that. He was attacking you, love. It doesn't matter that he can't defend himself. He deserves to have his junk destroyed. Now can we get back to this witch thing?"

"I was hoping that you would be distracted by vengeance and forget about that."

"Nope. When you hear someone call themselves a witch and then see them freeze a man, it tends to stick with you."

Maddy gave a heavy sigh. Sean knew that whatever she told him was going to change things between them, and he could only hope that it would change them for the better.

෫ඁ෬ඁ෭

Maddy never imagined that she would be having this conversation with Sean. "Hey, Sweetie, I'm a witch. Isn't that neat?"

Of course, maybe this was her chance to tell him why she did what she did. Maybe he would forgive her for being so terrible to him before.

"Can we deal with the frozen elephant in the room first?" she asked.

It was a stall tactic, but they also needed to do something about Reid. She wasn't sure how long he would stay that way.

"Do you have any rope or something to tie him up with?" he asked.

"Um, I'm sure there is something. Should we call the police?"

"Will you be able to unfreeze him before they come?"

Maddy shrugged. She didn't know if she could, or if she would be able to refreeze him if unfroze. The whole thing was kind of hit or miss for her.

"I think it would be better if we tie him up and maybe you should call Fiona. I'm assuming that she wouldn't be surprised to find a frozen guy in the living room or that you being a witch wouldn't be news to her?"

"No, it wouldn't. But it would be the first time there

was a frozen guy in the living room. I'm not exactly a practicing witch. Can I use your phone? Mine is in the kitchen."

Sean pulled out his phone and gave it to Maddy. She called Fiona who answered after a few rings.

"Hello?"

"Hey, Fiona, it's me."

"Maddy, why are you calling from Sean's phone? Is everything okay?"

"Well, yes and no. I'm okay now, but Reid attacked me at the house. I sort of froze him and now Sean and I are trying to figure out what to do with him."

"Sean?"

"Yes, he came into the house just as I announced that I was a witch and froze Reid. We are dealing with the Reid situation and then I will try and explain the witch thing."

"Well, I have something that might help with Reid. I've been over at Cassidy's this morning. She got some of her family's books, and we were looking through them. I found a spell that I think will reverse the Make Me a Match spell. It might make Reid leave you alone and, if it doesn't, then we can call the police and have him locked up. I just know that you will worry that it is somehow your fault if we had him arrested without trying something to break the spell."

"Okay, come over with the spell and I'll cast it. If it

doesn't snap Reid out of whatever his obsession with me is, then I will call the police."

"And then you will talk to Sean."

"Yes. I'm going to tell him everything." She looked over to where Sean was standing, watching her and smiling. He didn't look like he was freaking out over the witch thing and he didn't look like he was turned off by the idea that the girl he had said he was in love with might just be a witch. It gave Maddy hope that things might work out, after all. She got off of the phone and handed it back to Sean. "Fiona is coming home and thinks she knows something that will help with Reid."

"Good and I heard you promise that you are going to tell me everything. Do you think you could answer one question for me now?"

Maddy wasn't sure if she wanted to answer any questions he had to ask, but there was nothing she wouldn't do to try and mend their relationship. "Yes."

"Do you love me, Maddy?"

She didn't even have to think about the answer to that question. "Yes, Sean, I do love you. It has never been about do I love you or not. I have always loved you and always will."

Sean pulled her close then and wrapped her in his arms. He kissed her. It was a kiss that promised there would be a future and that the past could be just that—the past. At just that moment, Maddy heard movement from the living room and saw Reid coming at them with a face contorted with rage and hate. He pulled his arm back to hit Sean. Maddy held out her hands again and said very loudly, "Freeze again, motherfucker."

Reid froze, but the momentum of his body caused him to fall to the ground on his face.

"You are one bad ass witch, Maddy Simpson," Sean said and then he was kissing her again.

Maddy felt herself relax in his arms.

Fiona came rushing in and saw Reid lying on the floor of the living room. She quirked up one eyebrow at Maddy.

"He unfroze and tried to hit Sean," Maddy explained. "I was able to refreeze him."

"Okay. I brought the spell book from Cassidy's. We can do it fast, then you can unfreeze him and see if there is any change."

Sean looked confused. "Cassidy has a spell book? My sister knows that Maddy is a witch?"

Maddy really didn't want to get into it all until after they had dealt with Reid, but Sean deserved to know whatever he wanted to know. "I accidentally let it all spill to Cassidy the day we broke up. I was really, really drunk and was complaining about the stupid Make Me a Match spell and how I needed to know if your feelings were real. Then Fiona told her that there was some witch blood in your family and Cassidy started researching your family tree. It seems that your grandmother was a practicing witch, but that your mother did not have any sort of powers. Cassidy does, however. I'll tell you more later." Maddy turned to Fiona. "What do we have to do to cast this spell?"

"It's a pretty easy reversal spell. All you have to do is say the spell while clearing your mind of everything. We know you can do that. Then you need to read the Make Me a Match spell."

"I have it in my room in a drawer. I'll just run and get it."

Maddy ran and got the spell. She was hoping that this was the answer to everything that had been going wrong. She wanted to get this Reid stuff taken care of so she could focus of fixing what was broken between her and Sean. From the way he had been acting tonight, he should be willing to listen to her and give their relationship another chance.

She was back downstairs in less than five minutes. "I have the spell. Are we ready?"

Sean looked unsure all of a sudden. "Should I leave? Is this something I should be a part of?"

Maddy smiled at him and tried to act as if she wasn't nervous having him there watching her. "It isn't a big deal. I'm just going to read these things. As long as you don't make any noise or distract me, then you're more than welcome to stay." She took a deep breath. "In fact, I want you to stay."

Sean still didn't seem convinced that he should be there, but he sat on the couch and watched her.

Fiona handed Maddy the Walker Spell Book opened to the page with the reversal spell. Maddy placed it and the Make Me a Match spell next to each other on the table. Clearing her mind of everything she sat for a few minutes with her eyes closed, just thinking about nothing. Then she opened her eyes and read the spells.

Five minutes after opening the book, it was over. "Should I try to unfreeze him now?" she asked Fiona.

"I guess," Fiona answered with a shrug. "Sean, will you stand close in case we need your help."

Sean stood up and got closer to where Reid was lying, frozen on the floor. Fiona stood closer too, although Maddy had no idea what she would do if something were to happen.

"Okay, I'm going to unfreeze him now and see what happens." Maddy wiggled her fingers in Reid's direction and whispered for him to unfreeze.

Slowly Reid started moving and looking around Maddy and Fiona's living room. "What happened, Maddy? How did I get to your house?"

"You came over earlier. What is the last thing you remember, Reid?"

"I asked you out and you said yes, but then you wanted to meet earlier for coffee."

So he didn't remember the things that had happened since she had broken off their date at Crescent Coffee. That meant all of the threats and violence were some side effect of the spell and, now that she had reversed it, Reid was back to his normal self.

"I broke off our date and you got upset, but it is all over now. Fiona is going to take you home and we can talk more later if you want to."

Fiona led Reid out of the house and Maddy breathed a sigh of relief. She looked over at Sean, but he didn't look that relieved.

"What is the Make Me a Match spell, Maddy?"

Oh, shit. She didn't want to have to explain that to him, but she did owe it to him so that he would know the truth about everything that had happened and not just the bits and pieces that made her look good.

"Um, it's a spell I cast to find my true love. But it went wrong. I didn't cast it right, and instead of attracting my ideal man, I started attracting every man. That's why, when you moved back to Hollow Moon, I was dating a lot. I could break the spell's hold by declining a date with the man, but something went terribly wrong with Reid. He either had some sort of imbalance and the spell made it worse, or he was already fixated on me. But he seems better now that I reversed the spell."

"Why did you break up with me?"

Maddy swallowed and took a deep breath. Gone were the warm looks from earlier. Sean looked cold and shut off from her. "I couldn't be sure if you were under the spell or not. I needed to know if your feelings were real or if they were because of the Make Me a Match spell and the only way to do that was to break up with you."

"Why couldn't you talk to me about what was going on? Or were you just not planning on ever telling me about being a witch?"

Maddy wasn't sure if she would have ever told him, but she did know that she wouldn't have told him at this point in their relationship and she told him that.

Sean stood up. "I understand, at least I sort of understand, why you did what you did, Maddy. But I don't understand why you couldn't trust me. You should have been able to tell me what was going on and know that, while it would have taken some adjustment—I mean I wouldn't have believed the witch thing if I hadn't seen it with my own eyes and if I hadn't heard stories about my grandmother growing up. But what I'm having trouble with is that you didn't trust me at all, and I can't be with someone who doesn't trust me. I told you how hard it was for me to be in a relationship in the first place, but you were only worried about yourself and not how I would feel. I need to go."

Sean left her sitting there on her couch and went upstairs. Maddy didn't know what to do, but she knew that she didn't want Sean to leave without telling him one more time how much she loved him.

He came back downstairs with his bag packed. "I'm going to stay at Hank's for a few days. I'm not saying I won't be back or that I won't be able to get past this, but I just need a few days to digest all of this."

She stood and walked up to him. "I understand, Sean. I just want you to know that I do love you, so much. And that I'm so sorry for everything that I did wrong. If I could go back and do things differently I would—starting with never casting that stupid spell in the first place."

He kissed her cheek and walked out the door. Maddy sat back down on the couch and let the tears fall. He hadn't told her that he loved her back. Although she didn't deserve to know his feelings for her, she wished that he had at least given her some small bit of hope to hold on to.

Chapter 21

It had been seven days since Sean had left, and Maddy hadn't heard from him at all. Cassidy had seen him a couple times, so Maddy knew he was staying with Hank and that he was just as miserable as she was. Fiona and Cassidy were making her be sociable tonight, even though it was the very last thing she wanted to do. They were getting together for their usual Friday night margaritas and fictional boy talk.

Maddy hadn't read anything in the last few weeks and didn't even feel like talking about fictional men. All she wanted to do was sit in bed until Sean came back, but they weren't going to let her do that.

Cassidy was sitting on the foot of her bed. "Maddy,

did you get right into bed after you came home from work?"

"Maybe I did. I'm a grown woman and, if I want to go to bed at three in the afternoon, then I can go to bed at three in the afternoon."

"Don't you think that it is time for you to stop moping so much? I think that Sean is almost as pitiful as you, but that you are beating him by a smidge."

"Sean is pitiful?" Maddy asked, any mention of his name made her heart beat father.

"Yes, he's also moody, mean, and rude."

"I just want him to come back, Cassidy. I'm sorry for what I did, but I don't know what I can do to make it up to him. I apologized."

Fiona started to talk, but Cassidy beat her to it. "There isn't anything you need to do. It's up to Sean to figure out if he can get over what happened. You really didn't do anything that terrible, once you know why you did it. Sean just needs to get over it and I've told him so."

"Do you think it's the witch thing?"

"What? That he can't handle being with a witch? I don't think so. I was surprised by how easily he accepted all of that, but he told me that our grandmother used to do tricks for him when he was little. He also thought she was magical and, I guess, that made it easy for him to accept. Plus, seeing you freeze Reid in the middle of the living room, helped too."

Fiona spoke up then. "Speaking of Reid, he seems to be fine. No worse for the wear from the spell. In fact, I had coffee with him today and he was a perfect gentleman."

"Well, that's good. I'm glad that there doesn't seem to be any lasting desire on his side to hunt me down or turn the world against me for being a whore."

"No, he asked about you and Sean and said that he hoped the two of you worked things out."

Cassidy, who had been texting rapidly for the last few minutes, grinned at her phone. "Let's get you up and drunk."

Maddy got out of bed and both Fiona and Cassidy laughed at her choice of clothing. She was wearing a Wonder Woman nightshirt, complete with cape. "I needed some armor for our night of debauchery tonight. I thought Wonder Woman was a good way to ensure that I would be strong enough to make it through margaritas and guy talk with you two."

"Are you sure you don't want to put something else on?" Cassidy asked while still giggling.

"You've seen me wear silly pajamas before. Why does it matter what I wear tonight?"

"It doesn't. It's just that Fiona and I aren't wearing pajamas tonight and you are. I thought you might want to put regular clothes on so that you didn't feel like the odd man out."

"Nope. I will proudly wear my cape and fly around the room like a crazy woman once I've had too many drinks. I am in the mood to lose control just a little bit."

"Okay," Cassidy said.

Maddy thought that maybe there was more to Cassidy's desire to see Maddy in different clothes than just that she might feel uncomfortable, but she didn't really care at all.

The three friends headed downstairs and Maddy started making her margaritas. It was best that she made them. Maddy was in the mood to forget, so she made the drinks extra strong. It would only take one or maybe two to get everybody really drunk.

"So which fictional guy are we talking about tonight?" she asked as she gave Cassidy and Fiona their drinks.

"We thought tonight we would talk about a real man, instead of one from a book, or on TV or, in a movie."

"Really? We haven't done that in a long time. The only real guy we've talked about is Sean and I know there is no way that's who you are talking about. We just talked about him upstairs and I don't want to talk about him anymore tonight. There is nothing more to say than what we've already said."

"I was thinking we should talk about Hank," Fiona said.

"Hank?" Maddy asked and then she realized that Cassidy was blushing.

Maddy had been so caught up in herself that she just assumed everything was about her. Every conversation, every thought, was about her and her problems. It never entered her mind that something might be going on with Fiona or Cassidy.

"Yes, Hank. Hank and Cassidy to be exact. I saw them together the other day when I went to drop off something for Sean at Hank's apartment and things looked very cozy between the two of you. What was going on?"

"I was practicing a spell."

"A spell?" Fiona and Maddy both yelled out at the same time.

Maddy took a big sip of her drink and laughed. "What kind of spell were you practicing?"

"A spell called Kiss Me Now. Basically, you whisper an incantation and the object of your desire will kiss you."

"And you cast the spell with Hank?"

"Well, yeah. I mean I have had sort of a thing for him for a while and when he asked you out and you went on your half a date with him, I realized that I didn't like it. I want him for myself. So I thought I would try out the kiss me spell, see how it worked, and how it felt to be kissed by Hank."

"And how was it?" Fiona asked.

"It was amazing, but he freaked out afterward. He couldn't be kissing his best friend's little sister and there was no way I knew what I was doing. I'm too young and too inexperienced. Ugh, I don't want to talk about it." Cassidy took a big gulp out of her drink.

"So do you think you would want there to be something more between you and Hank?"

"I don't know. He thinks that I'm a little kid, but he didn't kiss me like I was a little kid. He kissed me like I'm a woman—a woman he desired more than his next breath. If he would kiss me like that and treat me like that all the time, I would be his in a heartbeat, but I won't put up with his I-can't-date- my-best-friend's-sister bullshit."

Maddy hated that she hadn't been paying enough attention to those around her to see what was going on. Sean had told her that he suspected that Hank had a thing for Cassidy and had for a long time, but Maddy had never thought that Cassidy might have a thing for Hank, too. Maddy wondered what else she had missed by paying attention to herself and not those around her.

They stopped talking about Cassidy and Hank, didn't even mention Sean and Maddy, and had barely touched on the subject of fictional hotties, when there was a pounding at the front door.

"Who could that be?" Fiona asked. "We weren't expected anybody, were we?"

Cassidy didn't answer, but she did smile.

Maddy turned to her and scowled. "Are you up to something, Cassidy?"

"I think you should get to the door, Maddy."

"I'm not getting the door, looking like this." Maddy wasn't crazy. She didn't know who was only the other side of the door, but she did know that she didn't want anyone to see her in her Wonder Woman pajamas.

"I really think you should," Cassidy said again.

The pounding continued and was getting louder. Fiona sighed and stood up. "I'll go get the door. I'm not wearing a cape, for goodness sake. Maddy, pour us more margaritas. I'm in the mood to dance and sing. I'll get rid of whoever is at the door, and we'll party."

Maddy got up and poured more margaritas, taking a liberal drink out of hers before topping it off again. She'd never made them this strong and she was already tipsy from the drink. It would be fun to dance and let go with Fiona and Cassidy for a bit.

"Maddy?"

"What, Fiona? I'm in the kitchen pouring drinks and getting some chips."

"The door is for you."

Maddy had no idea who it could be, but she decided that whoever it was could just deal with seeing her in her pajamas. She walked back into the living room and found Sean standing there, looking at her with his gorgeous green eyes. Time stood still and Maddy couldn't breathe for a few minutes.

"Hello, Maddy."

"Hi, Sean."

Fiona and Cassidy got up and moved toward the stairs. "We are going to head upstairs now so that you guys have privacy to talk about, um, whatever you might need to talk about," Cassidy said as she pulled Fiona toward the stairs.

Maddy ignored her. "Sean, I didn't expect to see you tonight."

He walked in and sat on the couch, holding out a hand to her so that she would sit next to her. She sat, trying to remain lady-like and maintain her distance, since she was wearing such a short night shirt. "You mean the cape and sexy pajamas weren't for me?"

Maddy laughed. "No, and I have a feeling that your sister must have known that you were coming. She tried to get me to change into something different, but I wasn't going to do that. I'm comfortable and had no idea that you were coming. Why are you here, Sean?"

"I want to talk to you." He shook his head. "No, that isn't true. The truth is that I couldn't stay away from you any longer. I needed to be with you more than I needed to breathe."

Sean pulled her close and crushed his mouth to hers. She wanted to tell him that he felt perfect against her and that she would never do anything to jeopardize their relationship again. It was more than she could articulate at that moment. She just held him close and tight.

"Maddy, I love you. I understand why you broke up with me. I really wish you had just talked to me, but I can't promise you that I wouldn't have reacted badly to hearing that you were a witch. I'm still not sure how okay I am with it, but we will work it out. I've just learned that I can't be without you."

"I don't want to be without you either."

He then pulled her back into his arms and kissed her. She kissed him back with all of the feelings that had been bottled up inside her for the last few weeks. She wanted to keep kissing him forever, but soon she heard Cassidy and Fiona coming back down the stairs.

"They are coming back down," she whispered against his mouth. "We can take this back to my room if you want to."

Sean smiled at her. "Oh, believe me, I want to. But there is something else I want more."

Maddy had no idea what he could want more than to spend the rest of the night in bed, making love, and reacquainting themselves with each other. "What's that?" she asked.

He laughed. "I promise it isn't bad."

He turned around, pulled something out of his jacket, then turned back around. "Maddy, I know that we've only been together for a blip of time. But I know, in my heart where it really matters, that we are meant to be together. I know the woman I love. The woman who I have spent the last twelve years talking to almost nightly on the phone, sharing my ups and downs with, is the woman I'm meant to spend the rest of my life with." He pulled out a jewelry box and opened it up while holding out his hand for Maddy's. Inside the ring box was a beautiful two-carat round solitaire diamond. It was gorgeous and Maddy couldn't believe that Sean was standing in front of her, holding it. "Madeline Simpson, will you do me the very great honor of marrying me?"

"Yes," she answered with tears in her eyes. "Yes, Sean, I will marry you."

Sean whooped loudly and put the ring on her finger.

Cassidy and Fiona came running in and screamed with joy. "Oh, my gosh!" Fiona yelled.

"I knew it," Cassidy screamed.

The whole time Maddy was looking at Sean and sharing a secret smile with him. She still wanted to be alone with him upstairs, but Cassidy and Fiona were already talking about getting out a bottle of champagne and celebrating.

Sean whispered to her, "We have a lifetime to be together, Maddy. We can wait a little while and celebrate with Fiona and Cass. I think maybe we should call Hank over, too. If that's okay with you."

"Okay, but I'm only willing to give everyone an hour or two before I'm stealing you away and taking you to my room."

"I'm counting on that."

୧୬୧୬

Sean was floating on cloud nine. Maddy had said yes to his proposal and their lives were finally on the right track again. Some would call him crazy for proposing after all that they had been through, but he knew they were meant to be together. He also knew that it was the only future that he was willing to trust in, and that he would do anything in his power to make sure that he and Maddy had a happy marriage that lasted forever.

He looked over at her, still in her Wonder Woman pajamas, dancing with Cassidy and Fiona, while drinking champagne, and looking at her engagement ring. Hank had arrived and was dancing with the girls. He had given Sean a surprised look when Maddy had shown him the ring, but had just congratulated them and started partying with the girls.

"Maddy, can you come here?" Sean called. He thought that he had shared her enough and it was time to take his fiancée somewhere where they could celebrate privately.

She sauntered over to him, a little tipsy and more

beautiful than a woman had a right to be. "Yes, fiancé of mine?" She leaned toward him and wrapped her arms around his neck.

He wrapped his hands around her waist and pulled her in tighter. "I was thinking that I might head up to bed. I'm tired and it's been a long time since I've been able to sleep in my own bed."

"I think I could go to sleep, too," she said with a sly smile.

Sean had a feeling he wouldn't be sleeping until the next morning and that was more than all right with him.

They said their goodbyes to Cassidy, Fiona, and Hank then headed upstairs. Maddy quickly stopped off in her bedroom to grab her blanket and pillow and then they walked the rest of the way up to the third floor and his bedroom.

"You know we could have stayed in your room."

"I know, but this puts even more distance between us and the rest of the party downstairs."

"That's true. I love you, Maddy."

"I love you too, Sean."

They got to his room and Sean didn't waste any time showing her just what he wanted to do with her. He swept her night shirt off over her head and laid her across the bed. He took a moment to look at her, lying gloriously naked across his bed, and thanked god that he was able to get over his own ego and come back to her. Then he set about showing her just how much he loved her and how much he'd missed her.

Epilogue

"Maddy, have you made the margaritas yet?"

"Yes, they are on the counter."

Maddy was sneaking back down the stairs from the third floor bedroom that she now shared with Sean. It was their bi-weekly girl's night at their house and Fiona had been bugging her for the last thirty minutes about making the margaritas. As Maddy passed Fiona's door it opened and Fiona walked out.

"So you made them and came back up here?"

Maddy blushed, but nodded. "Sean needed my help with something. He's getting ready to go out with Hank."

"Uh, huh. I'm sure he needed something," Fiona said with a knowing glance.

Maddy had worried about the transition of living in the house with just Fiona and her, then with Sean as a roommate, to Sean as a member of the family. It hadn't been an issue at all. Sean knew when to give Maddy and Fiona time alone, and Fiona seemed to sense when they needed couple time. It would all change if Maddy wanted to start a family, but that was a very long ways off.

They headed downstairs together and Maddy poured the first of what was sure to be several drinks. The door-bell rang and Cassidy came barreling in with Hank be-hind her. "I rang the bell to pretend I have manners, but then I walked in anyway." She grabbed a drink and sat down, giving Hank a go to hell look as he gave Fiona and then Maddy a kiss on the cheek.

Sean came down the stairs and twirled Maddy around while giving her another kiss. "I'm going to miss you."

"I'll miss you too, Sean."

Everyone made gagging sounds, but Maddy didn't care. The last six months had been the best of her life. She had gotten to know Sean even better than before and knew that there was no other man for her. And he felt the same way about her. He had encouraged her to learn more about being a witch and about who she could be if she embraced her heritage.

Cassidy, Fiona, and Maddy had been getting together weekly to learn about spells and how to do things that Maddy never imagined they would be doing six months earlier. She was loving every minute of it.

As she looked over at Cassidy and Hank, who were frowning at each other and trying to avoid the fact that they were meant to be together, Maddy started thinking that maybe it was time to cast a spell on them.

The End

About the Author

Married for almost thirteen years to her very own romance hero, Carrie Zimmerman spends most of her days writing while their three children are at school. Nights and weekends are spent watching the kids play soccer and summers are spent vacationing at the beach and playing outside. Zimmerman is so grateful to be doing something she loves that also allows her to spend time with her family whenever she can.

www.ingramcontent.com/pod-product-compliance
Lightning Source LLC
Chambersburg PA
CBHW071150170626
46809CB00002B/840